Alice has always been able to tell Cassidy anything . . . but what do you say to your BFF when you befriend her enemy?

Cassidy ran up to Alice. "Hey! It was weird not riding the bus with you. Did you get your reading done eventually?"

"Uh . . . yeah!" Alice said, deciding it would be awkward to say that she didn't without explaining why.

"Cool. Well, you're not the only overachiever on the street. I'm going to get some help with French during lunch, so I won't get to see you. I'll write you, okay?"

"I haven't had the chance to write yet," Alice confessed, handing Cassidy the notebook.

"No worries. . You've been busy!" Cassidy disappeared into her next class. But once the day was over, Alice didn't get the chance to get the notebook back and see what—if anything—Cassidy had written her. After ten minutes of craning her head, looking for Cassidy's smiling face to appear between the bus aisles, the doors shut, ferrying Alice back to her street—alone.

Why didn't she tell me she wasn't taking the bus home today? Alice wondered. *Maybe she was mad at me for not riding with her this morning. Maybe she had a doctor's appointment. Maybe she somehow knew I was talking to Nikki.*

But that last part was silly. Right?

More titles in the Picture Perfect series:

Book #1: Bending Over Backwards

Book #2: You First

PICTURE PERFECT

BEST
FRENEMIES

Cari Simmons and
Claire Zulkey

HARPER

An Imprint of HarperCollinsPublishers

Library of Congress Control Number: 2014952520

ISBN 978-0-06-231845-9

15 16 17 18 19   OPM   10 9 8 7 6 5 4 3 2 1

❖

First Edition

CHAPTER 1

THE FIRST DAY

"And where exactly do you think you're going?" Alice's mom called out.

Alice tried to suppress a smile, her hand on the latch as she pretended to leave for school.

"The bus stop?" Alice said, all innocence, turning away from the side gate as her mother stood on the back stoop, fists on her hips in pretend sternness.

"Not so fast," Mrs. Kinney said, and then she and her daughter grinned at each other. Alice's mom held up a silver camera dangling from her wrist. The two of them had played this little first-day-of-school game since Alice was in kindergarten, when she had begun to march off to the bus stop before learning that a) Kinneys always took photos on the first day of school and b) kindergartners don't walk to the bus stop. (Although freshly minted middle schoolers—which Alice was today—did!)

"Ready? Say cheese!" Mrs. Kinney said. Alice slumped her shoulders over, crossed her eyes, and stuck out her tongue, first-day-of-school zombie style.

"That pose doesn't really scream 'honors student,'" Alice's dad said, stepping outside with his mug of coffee and his shirt cuffs unbuttoned. Alice smiled, rolled her eyes, stood up straight, and re-posed in a more traditional manner, shaking her long red hair so that it flowed over her shoulders. Her parents could be embarrassing, but sweet—they were so proud of her for getting into honors classes, but really, it wasn't that big a deal. It's not like Alice set out to get there. It just . . . happened. Alice heard the fake-shutter sound of the digital camera, but then her mom kept holding the camera up for a few extra moments after taking the picture.

"Everything okay?" Alice asked.

"Oh, yeah," Mrs. Kinney said, and finally lowered the camera, emitting a tiny sniffle.

"Are you *crying*?" Alice asked in disbelief. "It's just school, Mom. I've done this before. School bus, pens, notebooks, teachers, remember?"

"I know," Mrs. Kinney said, laughing and running the side of her thumb below her lower eyelashes to collect any mascara that may have run. "It's just . . .

five seconds ago you were off to kindergarten. Now . . . middle school."

"*Honors* middle school," her dad said proudly, just as Alice heard the side gate latch. *Ugh.* Couldn't Cassidy have come at any other moment?

"Yes, *honors* middle school," Alice's best friend repeated teasingly, entering the Kinneys' backyard with her own mom behind her. Mr. and Mrs. Kinney beamed with pride, not realizing that there was the teensiest bit of tension between the two girls over this particular detail. Alice and Cassidy had been in the same class ever since the Turners had moved in across the street when the girls were five years old, but this year, while Alice had tested into honors, Cassidy . . . didn't. Alice knew Cassidy was supportive, but the whole thing still felt a little weird.

It wasn't that Cassidy wasn't smart: she had good grades and was funnier than Alice could ever hope to be. Alice just seemed to possess a little extra nerdiness when it came to school, and now, being separated from her best friend and being singled out in general for being "gifted" was her "reward."

Alice would have been just fine sticking with regular classes, especially since the honors thing had been a source of awkwardness between the two of them over the summer. While Alice said things like "I don't know how I'm going to make it without having you in my class! What if the other kids are mean? Or total dorks? Or worse, *totally mean dorks*?" Cassidy would say things like "Oh, you're *smart*, you'll figure it out," followed up by a hasty "I'm just kidding."

Alice knew, though, that they could move past it with just a bit of time. Being in separate classes just had to become the new normal. Alice needed Cassidy on her side the same way she knew Cassidy needed her, because middle school? Seemed a little scary.

"Cass, get over here," Alice said, yanking her friend over to pose in a first-day-of-school photo with her.

Cass patted the side of her head with her palm self-consciously. Over the summer she had made the very bold decision to cut off her shoulder-length braids and rock a short natural do. Her mom was thrilled.

"She said, 'Oh, honey, you look like me from the eighties!' and I swear she would have started crying a little bit if I didn't tell her to stop," Cass reported in her post-haircut debrief earlier that week. Of course, looking like your mom wasn't exactly at the top of the wish list of any self-respecting middle schooler.

However, with the haircut, Cass *did* look more

confident, more sophisticated. Alice knew for a fact that the new do was going to be a sensation, just like everything Cassidy did. *Everyone* wanted to be Cassidy's friend, boys and girls alike, but only Alice could count her as her best friend.

"I remember the first time you girls met." Cassidy's mom started to reminisce for probably the third time that week. Getting misty about old times was one of Mrs. Turner's quirks that Alice adored, along with the never-ending supply of cinnamon-flavored Jolly Ranchers in her purse and the zoomy little white convertible she drove, with the license plate that read HERS.

Mr. Turner was nice and all, but if Alice was going to get a ride home with Cassidy, she always hoped Mrs. Turner would show up in that convertible.

"Cassidy just toddled right up to Alice, who was playing in the front yard the day we moved in, and demanded, 'Let's be best friends,'" Mrs. Turner continued.

"Here she goes again," said Cassidy, rolling her eyes. Alice pretended to take a nap on her shoulder.

"And Alice said, 'Okay!'" Mrs. Kinney filled in. "'Okay!' Just like that."

"And you held hands and ran through the sprinkler

together. It was the most beautiful thing. And now look at you: best friends through all these years," added Mrs. Turner.

"Stop, you're going to get me going again!" Mrs. Kinney said, flapping her hands in front of her face.

"Mom, can you *please* just take the picture?" Alice asked. She actually didn't mind the reminiscing, but she sensed an impatient twitch in the golden-brown shoulders she had her arm slung over. It was time to get a move on and take this plunge, together.

Together—but only sort of, a glum voice in Alice's head said.

She couldn't help wondering whether Cassidy was, maybe, a little bit mad about her leaving the general track for honors. All summer long, Alice had tried to work up the courage to ask if she was okay about it. The last time she'd attempted to address it, she and Cass were picking their way across the beach near their house one late-summer evening. Lake Michigan was calmly lapping at their brightly painted toenails as the sun went down.

"So, with the honors class thing—" Alice ventured. (Okay, so she was also an honors-level awkward conversationalist.)

Cassidy cut her off. "It's fine!" she said in the same

bright-but-fake voice that Alice's mom used when she "wasn't mad" that Alice's dad hadn't put the laundry away. "We don't have to talk about it."

Alice clammed up, choosing to listen to Cassidy's words, even if she had a hard time ignoring her tone.

Now Mrs. Kinney snapped the photo and peered at it on the screen. "Another keeper!" she pronounced, and Alice smiled, although she wasn't surprised. She and Cassidy had plotted their first-day-of-school outfits the week before, making sure that they'd complement each other but not clash (or, heaven forbid, *match*). Alice wore a summery navy-and-white striped dress with a white jean jacket. It was already almost eighty degrees (North Shore summers lasted almost as long as its winters), but the air conditioning in the middle school, she had heard, could reach sub-arctic temperatures.

Cassidy, meanwhile, wore a bright red cardigan over a white T-shirt and black shorts with white polka dots on them. Alice would have looked like a little kid in them, but they showed off Cassidy's long, lean ballet-toned legs.

They agreed it would be okay if they both wore the gold sandals they had bought together earlier that summer, accented with fresh pedicures. Hey, even if they wouldn't spend every single second of school together, at least when they did, they'd look awesome— best friends ready to take on a new adventure.

"I couldn't sleep last night," Alice confessed, once they were on the bus. Cassidy turned towards her, eyes squinting from the sunlight reflecting off the sparkling lake. "But while I was tossing and turning, I came up with a stupendous plan!" Cassidy raised her eyebrows in amusement as Alice rummaged through her new backpack. It was oatmeal colored, with a design on the pocket that looked like a panda's head, with cute dark brown ears and everything. Alice relished the relative emptiness of the bag, when all she had rolling around in there were her new notebooks and school supplies and lip gloss; she had a feeling by the end of the day it would feel a lot heavier.

"Here it is!" Alice pulled out a purple notebook triumphantly. It was the perfect medium size, not so small that you couldn't write anything real in it, but just a *little* smaller than a regular school notebook (so a busy girl could find it just by feeling inside her locker or backpack).

"A notebook? Gee, you shouldn't have." Cassidy grinned.

"No, see, this is how we're going to stay in touch,"

Alice said. "Since we can't be in class together, we can keep each other up-to-date on everything that happens. Mean teachers, cute guys, gym embarrassments—everything!"

"I love it!" said Cassidy. "But do you think we'll have time for it? I mean, I'll have ballet and you'll be busy making Albert Einstein look like a chump."

"No, it'll be fun!" Alice said. "We don't have to write, like, *everything* down. Just fun little stories and jokes we hear and stuff. I'll give you my locker combination and you can give me yours, and we'll drop it off to each other between classes. It'll be like getting mail!"

Cassidy laughed. "Of course I'll do it. You do love your mail."

When she was six, Alice had embarked upon a master plan for getting new pen pals. She intended to float helium balloons with her name and address and a request for a postcard attached to the balloons' strings. She had visions of letters from Russia, Ghana, Indonesia—until her mother gently pointed out that the balloons were more likely to get stuck in the neighborhood trees or fall into the lake and strangle a duck. It turned out the only thing Alice loved more than getting mail was not feeling like a duck killer.

Gradually the bus filled up with kids. Cassidy and

Alice excitedly greeted the friends they knew from Comiskey Elementary and subtly eyed the students who came from other schools. Some of the girls looked nice; some of the guys looked especially cute; one girl with long, flowing dark curls and a tiny rosebud mouth glared at the floor and stomped down the bus aisle as if she didn't want to be there. Like it or not, Cassidy and Alice would be in classes with *all* these new kids. Time would tell who would prove to be friend or foe.

"I feel like we already have a *lot* of material for the notebook," Cassidy whispered with a sly grin once the year's cast of characters had assembled. Alice beamed and scribbled a quick kickoff note to Cassidy.

Maybe this will all be okay despite the fact that I'm being sent to nerd purgatory. Which should actually be called nerdatory. Portmanteau, right? Ugh, this is why I'm such a nerd in the first place! Happy first day of school . . . gulp!

CHAPTER 2

TROUBLE ALREADY

After a twenty-minute drive up Sheridan Road, past the dazzling array of large houses (each beautiful yet each distinct from the others in terms of style), the bus finally pulled up to Lakeside Middle School.

"Here we go," Cassidy said to Alice with a deep breath. "We got this!" Alice and Cassidy had discussed their initial middle school entrance several times over the summer. They would exit the bus in slow motion, the wind in Alice's hair and a wide, confident smile spreading across Cassidy's face as heads turned. "Who are *they*?" everyone would wonder, and make it a priority to befriend these two new, self-assured girls.

The reality was different, however. Nobody seemed to notice when Cass and Alice got off the bus, and they realized that slow motion was something that only happened in the movies and definitely not when the bus driver was telling you to get a move on.

The parking lot was a mob scene as it swarmed with students, all of whom seemed to know each other and were shouting to be heard above one another. A teacher with a clipboard stood in the crowd of kids like a rock stuck in a rushing river. She looked like she was imagining herself in another place, far, far away, as bright orange earplugs stuck out on either side of her head.

Alice wondered whether all these kids were really as confident as they seemed or if they were all faking it (well, maybe not the eighth graders: if she were in eighth grade, she'd swagger a bit too). She hoped at least one or two people, like her, were faking.

"Cassidy! Alice!" Alice turned to see Evie Gibson, April Searcy, and Xia Han—part of her and Cassidy's crew from elementary school—rushing towards them. For a few minutes before the bell rang, they oohed and aahed over each other's summer upgrades: Cassidy's haircut, Evie's cute clear-framed glasses, Xia's braces, and April's brand-new lack thereof.

"And what is this?" April asked, fingering Alice's panda backpack. "I want to adopt him and take him home and make him my best friend and name him George!"

Alice laughed at April's signature move, the over-the-top-gush.

A moment later, the girls followed the jet stream of students headed towards the double doors. Each one was being held open by two crabby-looking older teachers with matching sweat marks on their upper lips.

"A fancy backpack for fancy *honors* homework," Evie teased, giving her shoulder a friendly squeeze.

"Yeah, you ready to rock this? I heard that in honors you get an exam on the first day," said Xia as the girls let the big school swallow them up. *An exam? Great. Here we go,* thought Alice, trying to be brave.

"Hey, Evie, what was horseback-riding camp like?" Cassidy asked, changing the subject. "Did you ride horses the *entire* time?" She grinned at Alice and winked. Cass knew talking about honors made her embarrassed—and caused her to blush redder than Cassidy's cardigan—to talk about honors classes and brains in general. Maybe after she'd settled into honors classes, she'd feel okay about talking about it more, but for some reason it just made her bashful, even though she knew Cassidy wanted to cheer her on as much as possible, despite the potential awkwardness.

"Yeah, like, did you eat dinner while you rode a horse?" asked Xia, laughing.

"Did you *sleep* on a horse?" April asked.

They're all going to be in class together and I'll be solo,

Alice thought. *They'll keep joking around without me.*

As if reading her best friend's nervous thoughts, though, Cassidy handed the notebook back to Alice.

"I wrote down my locker combo in it," Cassidy explained with a smile. "So you can put the notebook in there when we can't meet up. Write down yours so I can give it back to you after you write to me."

"Thanks," Alice said, grateful that she already had a little something from Cassidy to get her through her first class.

The second bell rang, but instead of feeling brave with Cassidy's locker combination in her hand, Alice felt a surge of panic, especially as she saw April, Evie, and Xia start to drift to the classroom across the hall from where she would be.

"I'm nervous," Alice whispered into Cassidy's ear, decorated by a gold-pink shiny ball. She caught a whiff of the delicious-smelling coconut oil that Cassidy put in her hair.

"You'll be great!" Cassidy said. "Awkward mom high five?"

The girls performed the weird stiff-armed high five they'd seen their own moms do a million times. "Yeah!" Cassidy cheered, and gave a double thumbs-up. Alice laughed. Her best friend always knew how to cheer her up on the outside, even if she was still a little uncertain on the inside.

Unlike out in the school yard, the kids in Ms. Garrity's homeroom looked a lot more like Alice felt—nervous and unsure—which made her feel better. Plus, she spotted a few kids in her class who she knew from elementary school, like Christy Gillespie, with her short blond springy curls. Alice had always admired her for being supersmart but incredibly friendly. "I love your earrings, Christy!" Alice said as she passed by Christy's desk, complimenting the little panda-shaped studs with tiny pink hearts on their bellies.

"Bears are so in right now!" Christy said, nodding at Alice's backpack.

Okay, Alice thought. *So maybe this won't be so bad.*

Alice didn't want to look picky, so she grabbed the first empty desk she saw and pulled out a (regular-size) notebook and pen. A dark-haired boy seated next to her smiled uneasily.

"Can I confess something?" he leaned over and asked after a moment.

"Sure," Alice said.

"I'm totally nervous," he said. "I kept having dreams all week that they put me in the wrong class and I failed everything. Do you think that's normal?"

Alice nodded. "None of my good friends from last year are in this class, and I've been freaking out about not knowing anyone."

He smiled. "I'm Aaron Woolsey."

"Alice," she said. "Alice the nerd."

Aaron laughed. "And you can call me Aaron the geek. Tell me something I don't know—oh, wait, you can't, because I'm *so smart!*" he joked.

Alice grinned as the final bell rang and Ms. Garrity stood at the front of the class to read attendance.

Christy's nice, Aaron is funny, so maybe it's all going to be okay, Alice thought. She let her eyes wander around the room, relaxing into the idea that in a few weeks she'd know everyone's names, even the people she'd never seen before. *Everyone seems pretty normal,* she thought. But then her eyes landed on the mean-looking girl from the bus. She looked up at the same time, making eye contact with Alice. Her frown deepened.

Maybe she was just nervous, like everybody else! Alice smiled, newly full of confidence after cute and nice Aaron's friendly conversation, but the curly-haired girl just narrowed her eyes and pointedly looked ahead at Ms. Garrity. It was if her eyeballs had said, "Don't even think about it."

Oh no.

"You guys probably know all this stuff already, but we're going to go over it, just for fun," said Ms. Garrity sarcastically as she flipped open a manila envelope and began to run down the school policies. Alice gave herself permission to zone out, pulling out the purple notebook and opening to its first promising blank page, feeling reassured by the ♥ *you!* note Cass had written beneath her locker combination on the inside of the front cover.

She glanced up at Ms. Garrity, who was wearing an unflattering khaki skirt cut to a weird place on her legs, above the ankles and below the knee. Even Alice's mom, who wore yoga pants like it was her job, would call the skirt "unfortunate." Ms. Garrity continued to read the announcements almost comically loudly and slowly, as if she were just killing time and couldn't stand to have to actually look at or speak with the students.

That gave Alice a brilliant idea: if she could paint a clear picture of what her homeroom was like for Cassidy, and Cass did the same for her, they wouldn't feel that far apart after all. And if they ever exchanged funny stories about what happened in class, they could each perfectly picture what happened.

Alice drew a grid on the page and started

diagramming a funny seating chart of the kids in the class. She illustrated Christy Gillespie's seat with flowing curlicues, then noted "Cute! Nice!" next to Aaron Woolsey and described the kids she hadn't met yet with words like *Hawaiian-shirt kid*, *too-strong-perfume girl*, and *shoes I want to steal*.

Alice wrote *Me!* inside the square that indicated her desk, and doodled a little panda on the edge to indicate her backpack. When she got to the mean-looking girl's seat, Alice scribbled a frowny face with a dark V between her eyes to indicate her furrowed brow. The effect was funny. Alice had to suppress a giggle.

"I said, did you hear me, Alice Kinney?"

Alice was jolted out of her illustration. It felt like her armpits went from dry to nervous and sweaty in one second.

"Excuse me?"

"I appreciate that you're taking notes so studiously, but it's really not necessary in homeroom," said Ms. Garrity, who really seemed like she was in a really bad mood for so early in the year. She leaned against her desk and crossed her clog-clad ankles as if she were already exhausted. "What I was asking is whether you knew if your parents were going to be providing us the permission slip for you to participate in biology labs."

"Oh. Yes," Alice said in a tiny voice. Her face was burning up so much she was tempted to touch it to see if it was as hot as it felt. The other students stared at their desks, probably thinking, *I'm glad that wasn't me.*

"Great, thanks for letting me know," said Ms. Garrity, diving back into her announcements.

Out of habit, Alice glanced to the seat on her right, which was where Cassidy used to sit when they were in homeroom together last year, when everything was easy and made sense. Whenever anything funny used to happen in class, Alice would glance over so she and her best friend could laugh together, like the time before Christmas break when they secretly added a tiny cap and beard to the stuffed duck Mr. Shears kept in his science lab and everyone in the class noticed, one by one, except for Mr. Shears. Or whenever she or Cassidy got in trouble (like the time they got chided for disrupting Mr. Shears's class, even though they could totally tell he thought it was funny too), they'd perfected the art of sneaking a quick look to each other for reassurance.

However, this time Alice found the opposite of reassurance: with Cassidy being in the other room, her glance fell again on the dark curly-haired girl from the bus, who stared at Alice and rolled her eyes before fixing her gaze pointedly to the front of her room, as if to say, "It's not *that* hard to pay attention, is it?"

Alice looked back miserably at her desk, yearning to write about this already to Cassidy, but obviously, she couldn't. She was stuck, both in her seat and in this dumb smart-kid class. Why did things have to change? Was it too late for her to move back down to regular classes? What did that girl have against her, anyway?

CHAPTER 3

HONORS STUDENTS FINISH LAST

"So," Cassidy asked, bumping her hip against Alice's as the two girls stood in the school parking lot. They were fifty percent waiting for the bus, fifty percent trying not to look too obvious as they scoped out the football team stretching on the field next to the lot. "Was it better than a poke in the eye with a sharp stick?"

Alice smiled and raised her hand to her forehead to create a visor against the golden afternoon sun. It was so unfair that school always started during the most beautiful time of year.

"You know, it wasn't all bad," Alice admitted, and it was true. Everything had been smooth sailing after the embarrassment of homeroom. "My English teacher might not actually be evil." English was taught by Mr. Nichols, a wiry, energetic young teacher with twinkly brown eyes and rolled-up shirtsleeves and a funny type of sarcasm.

"Well, I hope you all like reading, because we're going to do a lot of it this year," Mr. Nichols had announced, handing out copies of To Kill a Mockingbird to the class. Alice felt like she had caught a break there—she and her parents had listened to the audiobook a few summers ago on a road trip down south. (Perhaps being nerdy was hereditary.)

Alice had loved To Kill a Mockingbird so much that they had rented the film version as soon as they got home, and she had developed a bit of a secret crush on Gregory Peck, the actor who played the handsome and good hero of the story, Atticus Finch. . . . although it was something she would never, ever tell anyone—not even Cassidy. So Alice looked forward to actually reading the book, and she hoped that meant that she'd have a pretty easy time with the work that came with it.

Mr. Nichols gave them a list of some of the other books they'd be reading in class, and while Alice hadn't heard of a lot of them, they had exciting, adult-sounding titles like Lord of the Flies and Brave New World.

After English was math, which came easy to Alice in a way that she couldn't explain. She just understood it, which thrilled her parents, since they both had stopped taking math classes after high school. Sometimes when they were out to dinner, they let her figure out how much to tip their waiter. Her dad had even mused once over the breakfast table that summer, "You know, I bet you could handle taking some math classes at the high school."

"NO!" Alice replied so loudly that he put his hands over his ears. Being in honors classes was enough. She didn't need to head across town to the huge, scary high school, which was overrun by football players who probably ate middle schoolers for lunch. Actually, not even for lunch—just for a snack.

"It's okay if she's just in the grade she's in," Alice's mom cut in, reassuring her.

Mr. Sellke, bearded and full of a geeky sort of excitement that only math teachers could pull off, tried to recruit volunteers for the math team with terrible puns ("I think you would all make great *additions* to the team!"). Alice kept her head down and tried to make herself invisible. Just because she was good at math didn't mean she wanted to make it her hobby. Plus, if she got signed up for math team, with its after-school practices, she'd *never* see Cassidy.

Alice hid behind her red curtain of hair and wrote a note to Cassidy (*Very important question: Did you ever notice that "geometry" sounds like "Gee, I'm a tree"?*)—

"Great! We have a new team member!" Mr. Sellke

cheered. Alice turned to see the sour-faced, curly-haired girl from the bus and homeroom (whose name, Alice had learned, was Nikki Wilcox), with her hand up. She *would* volunteer for one of the least fun things. She probably also loved cleaning her room, putting away dishes, and eating overcooked asparagus.

The first day was also made easier by lunch, since it was the one period where Alice got to hang out with Cassidy and her other elementary school friends. After biology, Alice entered the raucous cafeteria, nervously glancing from table to table at groups that had either known each other from elementary school or somehow had already bonded in the first few hours of school. She held her breath until her eyes finally landed on Cassidy, who waved to Alice so hard it looked like her arm was going to fall off. "Alice! Over here!" She had saved a table for their friends from Comiskey to sit together, and Alice was grateful that, thanks to her best friend, she didn't have to wander around the cafeteria like she was lost in the wilderness.

"First things first," Cassidy said as she dramatically rolled back the foil on their hot lunch. "What on earth is this?"

"Hmm," said Alice, examining the brown lump

surrounded by little green balls of what was presumably poison. "It may have been an animal at one point. A long, long time ago. Ice age, maybe?"

"Do you dare me to take a bite?" asked Cassidy, who put a molecule of the meatish substance on her fork.

"EEEW!" screamed the girls as Cassidy tried it.

"Mmm, squirrel," Cassidy joked. "Delicious." She rolled the foil back up while the other girls groaned. Then she turned to Alice. "So how's your first day going so far?"

"Okay," said Alice. "We'll see. Most people seem pretty cool so far, except this one girl, who looks like she wants nothing to do with the rest of us."

"That curly-haired girl from the bus?" asked Cassidy. "Maybe she's just having a bad day. Maybe she heard about the hot squirrel lunch ahead of time."

"Probably." Alice laughed. "We'll see. How about you?"

"Okay so far!" Cassidy said brightly. "It helps to have these troublemakers in class with me," she said, gesturing to Evie, April, and Xia. "I don't know how I'd survive in class with a bunch of new people. You're brave, Alice!" she said, and Alice blushed. She didn't feel very brave, but Cassidy bolstered her.

"Hey, Cassidy!" said a girl Alice didn't recognize. "Maybe eat lunch with us sometime?" She gestured to a table full of kids from another grade school, who waved.

"Sure thing, Maddie!" Cass said. "Have you met my best friend, Alice, by the way? She's in honors classes."

"Ooh, a smarty-pants!" Maddie said, raising her eyebrows, impressed. "Well, see you in French, Cass!"

Cassidy crossed her eyes and stuck out her tongue at the mention of her least-favorite subject.

"Yeesh, we've only been in school for a few hours and you're making friends already?" Alice said. She felt proud (and maybe a tiny bit envious) of Cassidy's ability to talk to everyone. Alice made an effort to be outgoing, but she could never be as popular as Cassidy, who had an almost magical ability to make everyone around her want to be near her.

The summer before, at lake camp, even the counselors wanted to be pals with Cassidy, admiring her cute straw beach tote and how well she handled a canoe. The Lake Michigan fish probably would compliment her on her swimming form, if they could.

"You just make me look good," Cassidy told Alice. "Now let's talk about the important stuff," she announced to the table. "I heard there's a bowling alley in the basement of the school that only four people in the entire building have access to. Did you guys hear that?"

The girls buzzed over this gossip, along with the announcement that there was going to be a pep rally in October. (Would they go? Was it going to be lame? Or cool?) There were also whispers of a fight in the west wing during second period, and a discussion of the terrible decision of somebody on the school staff to make the girls' gym uniforms red and pink. Blech!

After lunch, Alice felt invigorated by the positive energy from Cassidy and faced the rest of the day with confidence. The classes seemed manageable, the kids in her classes seemed mostly human, and before she knew it, she was back on the bus, heading home. *One day down.*

Alice smiled to herself as she gazed out the window at the tiny golden leaves still hanging on to the trees. The bus turned back onto Sheridan Road to take her home. In a month or two, those leaves would be shaking off the trees, falling down on the students' heads like sunshiny confetti.

"Cassidy, did you see what Ms. Haynes was wearing

in social studies?" Tess Sawyer, one of the girls on the route, asked, leaning across the bus aisle, her delicate gold T necklace hanging off her neck and swaying in space.

"I *know*! It was amazing!" Cassidy said. "Were those bananas on her dress, or was that just a yellow-and-black design?"

"I think we should ask her next time she wears it." Tess grinned.

"And her boots were super cool too. I didn't know teachers would ever wear, like, tough-guy boots like that," said Cassidy.

"They look like my sister's Doc Martens," Tess said. "Maybe I'll steal them from her closet."

"What if we all ended up dressing like Ms. Haynes?" Cassidy said. "I can't decide if that would be hilarious or tragic."

"My homeroom teacher was wearing the saddest skirt and shoes," Alice offered up. "She was in a really bad mood too—maybe it's because she needs a make-over." Cassidy and Tess laughed politely and then went back to gushing over Ms. Haynes and her long dread-locks. Cassidy fingered her own hair as if contemplating copying Ms. Haynes herself.

Alice could feel her smile fading a bit. She couldn't

help but feel a little bit bummed that a) she was missing out on this cool social studies teacher and b) she was at a loss for conversation. Alice glanced around the bus to see if anyone from honors classes was on the route with her, but the only person she could find was Nikki Wilcox, way in the back, ignoring everyone around her as she leaned over *To Kill a Mockingbird*.

Finally the big yellow bus pulled up to Cassidy and Alice's street, and the girls got off. Alice breathed in the lake air and glanced at the planters at the front of the block that Mrs. Turner kept filled with seasonal flowers. It always made the street feel like a special, cheery place. Right now the planter was brimming with bright yellow chrysanthemums, round and spiky like miniature stars, to welcome Alice and Cassidy back home.

"You want to come over? My mom was on a baking tear last night!" Cassidy offered.

Barring any big projects, illnesses, or vacations, the girls *always* spent an hour or so together after school, eating snacks and discussing the day. It was what kept their friendship strong after all this time.

"Of course I do," Alice said, already dreaming of Mrs. Turner's caramelly turtle brownies.

"You sure you don't have too much *homework* or something, honors kid?" Cassidy teased, but Alice's shoulders slumped beneath her backpack straps.

"Actually . . . I do," Alice said, remembering *To Kill a Mockingbird* and all the other little tasks she had been given for the next day. They hadn't seemed like a lot one at a time, but she had more work than she realized—and it felt weird to blow it off so early.

It didn't seem right. Wasn't the first day of school just supposed to be sort of a joke day or something?

"Oh, that stinks, I'm sorry," Cassidy said. "I was just kidding around. I didn't mean to—"

"No, it's okay," Alice said. "Maybe if we just hang out for a minute—"

"Alice, we'll catch up soon, don't worry," Cassidy said. "You don't want to fall behind already! Besides, isn't that what the notebook is for? So we can keep up?"

"You're right," Alice said. She pulled the notebook out of the panda bag, which barely felt any lighter. "I already got in trouble today."

"I would expect nothing less from you, you rebel," Cassidy said. They had reached her parents' driveway, paved with bricks with little bright green tufts of moss poking through. Alice yearned to walk up the drive to Cassidy's house and flop on the comfy cream leather couch like always, but her best friend was right: she couldn't fall behind on her very first day.

"Well." Cassidy shrugged. "See you tomorrow morning, I guess."

"Okay." Alice sighed and walked back to her house.

"Hey hey!" greeted Alice's dad, turning away from salad-making duties when she walked through the door. "You made it alive!" He held up a hand for Alice to high five, which she hit halfheartedly. "Ow!" he said, pretend-rubbing his hand on his pants in pain. Alice was *not* in the mood for his sense of "humor."

"How was your first day, honey?" Alice's mom asked, rolling her eyes at Mr. Kinney. "I made you a nice little snack." She gestured to the wooden kitchen table, which was laid with a blue ceramic bowl filled with mixed berries. Alice threw her bag on the alcove bench that overlooked the backyard and pulled a seat up to the table. Her mom brought her a glass of ice water, auburn wisps that had escaped her ponytail framing her face.

"So tell us all about it!" Alice's dad pulled up a chair and grabbed a giant strawberry. Mrs. Kinney expertly slid a plate beneath him to catch any drips.

"Oh," said Alice, wanting to be polite but not quite in the mood to be chatty. She was still bummed from not being able to go over to Cassidy's house, plus she had that stupid homework to do. "You know."

"We did know, once," said Alice's mom, gazing at Mr. Kinney quizzically. "But we forgot."

"We are old," Mr. Kinney said. "Middle school was a long time ago for us."

"Dinosaurs and all, chiseling homework into rock slabs," Mrs. Kinney said. "So humor us."

"There were a few kids in my homeroom class who I knew from Comiskey. Our homeroom teacher, Ms. Garrity, was in a really bad mood," Alice said, deciding not to mention the part where she got called out for not paying attention.

"Probably because she had to get off the beach and teach a bunch of lousy kids," Mr. Kinney joked.

"She doesn't seem like someone who spends a lot of time on the beach," Alice said. "Anyway, I met some of the other kids and most are okay. One is kind of weird, though. Stuck up or something, I don't know. She gave me some mean looks."

"She's probably just nervous," Mrs. Kinney suggested, always trying to see the best in people, even those she'd never met before.

Alice told them about the rest of the day, her parents pausing to ask questions and clarify along the way, like they were going to write a report on her. Sometimes being an only child meant getting a little bit *too* much attention.

"Anyway," Alice said. "The real bummer is that I actually have homework to do tonight. I really wanted to see Cassidy and catch up, but I have to read *To Kill a Mockingbird*."

"But you've read it before," Alice's dad pointed out.

"Yeah, but it was a while ago," Alice said. "I'm sure there's stuff I forgot."

Alice's mom and dad shared a look.

"You'll see Cassidy plenty," Mrs. Kinney reassured her, running her hand through Alice's hair and twirling a red-gold tendril in her fingers. "I know it feels hard right now, but you'll figure it out and it'll get better, I promise."

"I hope so," Alice grumbled. After bringing her plate to the sink, she shouldered her backpack, which somehow felt heavier than when she took it off.

"Or else what?" her dad teased, and she threw him a foul look as she climbed the navy carpeted stairs to her room.

"Dinner at six, okay?" Alice's mom called up to her.

Alice could only muster an "uh-huh" in response.

In Alice's room, which was done up with peach floral wallpaper and turquoise carpeting, the sun shone cheerily through the white-painted shutters. Just because school had started, summer was still not technically over. *What a tease,* Alice thought. She dumped the contents of her backpack onto the floor and sighed, picking up her paperback copy of *To Kill a Mockingbird* and her school planner, already filled with a list of tasks.

She contemplated turning on the radio to lighten her mood but knew she'd never really be able to concentrate on reading without complete silence, so she settled onto her bed with the white fluffy duvet cover and cracked open her book. Outside, she could hear kids running around, screaming happily in their backyards, and in the distance, the sound of motorboats on the lake. One day down: the whole rest of the school year to go.

CHAPTER 4

TOGETHER AGAIN

"Here's you on the first day," Cassidy said, gearing up to do one of her impressions of Alice, which were never accurate but always hilarious. She balled her hands up into tiny fists and rubbed them at her eyes like a baby. "Waah! I'm so scared! I'm Alice Kinney and I'm so smart and so cute and because of this I'm going to have a terrible time at school! Boo hoo!"

"Yeah, well here's you." Alice grinned, standing up and tucking her denim skirt between her thighs so that it resembled shorts. "I'm Cassidy! Look at my shorts! I've got long, skinny legs, woo woo!" She did a few high kicks for emphasis as she ran her hands over her scalp. "How's my hair? How would you rate it on a scale of fabulous to extra-fabulous?"

It was Friday night, and Alice had to laugh about how freaked she had been the first day of school. That

Monday, it took her less than an hour to get all her homework done, and she realized that as long as she was disciplined about getting home in time, she could still go over to Cassidy's house—and had gone twice already in the last week.

"To our first week," Cassidy said, raising a glass of the special infused water Mrs. Kinney liked to experiment with. Sometimes it was delicious. Other times she left some jalapeño peppers in the water for too long, and Alice and her dad had the comical yet painful experience of drinking *hot* but *cold* water.

This batch, though, flavored with fresh plums and cinnamon sticks, was a winner. Alice clinked glasses.

"Hold on, I've got a great idea," Alice said, scrambling to her feet and going to her white drafting table, the organization of which was her pride and joy. Alice loved finding the perfectly sized box, jar, bowl, or odd container to hold her desk supplies. She opened up a drawer on a tiny clear plastic chest and pulled out a sheet of metallic gold stickers, the kind teachers put on good projects and papers. Alice liked to decorate cards and letters with them.

"I figured we could look back at the notebook and put stickers next to the best entries," she said. "That way, if we're ever sad or bored or something like that, we know which ones to look back on so we can laugh."

"I like it," Cassidy said, nodding. "Make sure you put in that one story you told me about that kid who set himself on fire."

"Oh my goodness, poor Todd," Alice said, laughing.

After all the permission slips had finally been turned in, nobody had been more excited about going into biology lab and "messing stuff up" than Todd Tian, who Alice was sure was either secretly a pyromaniac or a future mad scientist.

Not ten minutes had passed since the students had filed into the lab when the students heard "Uh, Ms. Crawford?" from the back of the room. The students and the teacher all turned around to see Todd, in his protective apron and glasses (which he had made fun of for being "weak," because it was required that the students wear them each lab, even if they were just growing mold on Jell-O), looking down with alarm at a small but persistent flame that crept up his apron like a friendly snake.

Todd was physically fine (once Ms. Crawford, astoundingly cool under pressure, had thrown a fire blanket over him), but he was suspended from participating in labs for two weeks *and* any time he drew attention to himself in class, he was teased with people saying, "Uh, Ms. Crawford? Do you have a fire extinguisher?" or "Uh, Ms. Crawford? Do you think I'm hot?"

If he was lucky, people would forget about it by high school, but Alice hoped he wasn't ruling out the possibility of leaving town and changing his name to completely escape it.

"You guys got to play with fire in your first week?" Cassidy asked.

"That's the hilarious thing," Alice said, putting a sticker next to the Todd story and illustrating it with a red pen. She drew flames coming out of it. It was rather beautiful, actually. "We weren't. We're studying ocean currents this week. We still haven't figured out where or how he did it."

"Well, I'm jealous," said Cassidy.

"Jealous that you didn't set yourself on fire?"

"No, that you guys even have access to fire," Cassidy said. "Do you know what we're doing in *our* bio lab? Growing bean sprouts! And I don't think we're even allowed to touch the sprouts. We just get to look at them and maybe measure them."

"Well, if you're lucky, maybe you'll get to eat them too," Alice joked.

"Dear diary, today I ate a bean sprout. It was the

best day of my life," Cassidy said dreamily. She grabbed the notebook and flipped through it.

"Ooh," she said, stabbing a robin's-egg-blue-painted fingernail at the page where Alice had drawn the seating chart the first day. "Nikki Wilcox. Did I tell you that she's in my ballet class?"

"*She's* in ballet?" Alice asked in disbelief. After watching Cassidy dance, and seeing the way she lit up the stage with her smiling eyes and graceful dips and jumps, Alice couldn't even picture Nikki participating in something so fun or pretty as ballet. Alice would love to dance herself, but she had the coordination of a moose, plus she suffered from crippling stage fright, ever since a recital in third grade when she went to play the piano and discovered, to her horror, that the piano hadn't been tuned.

She had played the Mozart minuet perfectly, but it sounded like she was playing it with her elbows. She had gone and cried in the bathroom for an hour afterwards.

"Yes, she is," Cassidy confirmed. She stuck her legs out and began stretching, the way she did whenever ballet came up in conversation. Alice couldn't decide which was more impressive, Cassidy's flexibility or the floral-pattered leggings she was wearing. "She's not bad either, so far that I can tell, but she always has a stank face on."

"Stank face?" Alice laughed.

"I heard an eighth grader say that," Cassidy confided. "You know, it's like when you look like you smell something bad?"

"Like this?" Alice said, screwing up her face like she had just smelled her mom microwaving fish taco leftovers.

"Like this!" Cassidy said, pinching up her nose and mouth as close together as she could in the middle of her face. The girls dissolved into laughter again.

"After class," Cassidy said, "a bunch of us hang out afterwards and just have a little snack while we get dressed. No big deal, just like orange slices or whatever. But not Nikki—not only does she not spend time with the class, she just busts right out without saying good-bye or even changing. It's like she can't stand to be in the same room as us for one second longer than she has to!"

"I wonder what's up with her," Alice said.

"Who knows?" said Cassidy. "Let's talk about something fun. Speaking of eighth graders, there's a boy who's kind of cute who I think might actually know I exist."

"Oooh, tell!" Alice said, flopping on her stomach on her bed.

"His name is Jesse, and he's on the baseball team with David," Cassidy explained, referring to her older brother. "So I see him when my mom picks David up after practice. He's really skinny, but he has the cutest smile," she said, looking dreamy.

"Nice!" said Alice. "And you think he likes you?"

Something about the phrase "cutest smile" made a picture of Aaron Woolsey pop into Alice's head. She shook it away. She had decided to keep crushes on hold for now—it was hard enough to deal with middle school and honors classes. Sure, it was fun to talk to Aaron in class and to see him smile, but she was okay with just being friends with him—for now.

"Well, he always seems to make a point of smiling at me when we pick David up," Cassidy said, pulling out a pink heart-shaped lip balm from her pocket and applying it—like the guy in question was going to show up and ask for a smooch then and there. "*And* he said hi twice to me so far this week in the hall at school."

"Wow, Cassidy," teased Alice. "It sounds like you guys are practically engaged already!" In elementary school Cassidy had had a tendency to crush hard and fast on boys—so fast that sometimes she didn't have a

Boy of the Week but a Boy of the Hour.

"Oh, hush your butt!" Cassidy said, hitting Alice with a pillow. The girls laughed and spent the next half hour playing the catalog game: taking a pile of some of the most random catalogs Alice's parents received and choosing one thing from each page that they'd *have* to buy.

This was a good week for catalogs. Alice's parents had received one selling strange, seemingly useless gizmos like automatic dog feeders and leg massagers; another that apparently thought Alice's parents were ninety years old, as it featured gadgets to help old people zip up their clothes and pick things off shelves. The best one, however, displayed high-end Halloween costumes for dogs. Before Cassidy had to go home for dinner, they had picked out some quite elaborate outfits for Bagel, Cassidy's pug, who was in danger of being dressed as a dinosaur, a Raggedy Ann doll, and possibly a mermaid—or was it mer-dog?

"Pizza for dinner tonight okay?" Mrs. Kinney said, poking her head into Alice's room after Cassidy had gone home for the night.

"Sure!" said Alice.

"You seem happy," said Mrs. Kinney, sidling her way inside.

"Well, you see, I like pizza," explained Alice. "It tastes good in my mouth."

"No, I mean in general. You seem a lot cheerier than you did at the beginning of the week."

"I guess I was just nervous about school, and about not seeing Cassidy as much," said Alice.

"And it turns out that both are more manageable than you thought, right?"

"We'll see," said Alice. "I don't want to jinx anything."

"I told you it wouldn't be so bad," said Mrs. Kinney, grabbing and flipping through the old-people catalog. "Yikes, please tell me that I'm not this ancient yet."

"Not for about four more years," said Alice.

"Will you promise to rub my poor bunions?" Mrs. Kinney asked in a creaky old voice.

"Don't you have a pizza to order, Mom?" Alice smirked.

"Yeesh! If a mother can't ask her favorite daughter to perform basic foot care, who can she ask?" joked Mrs. Kinney, and left to rifle through the menu drawer. In a minute, she'd quiz Alice's dad on what he'd like to order, even though they always agreed on one pepperoni pizza and one spinach stuffed.

Alice sat on the floor, propped up a pillow at the base of her bed, and picked up the purple notebook again, flipping through it and noting with satisfaction the hilarious stories that she and Cassidy had already begun accumulating. The notebook was one of her best ideas ever! It was going to be so fun to look back on it later, maybe even years from now.

But the part of her brain that couldn't help but notice patterns started pinging: the entries in the last week seemed to get shorter and shorter with each day—particularly Cassidy's. The first day's entry took up ten lines, then Tuesday's, eight, while Friday's was a mere three lines long. What if the notebook ended up withering and dying because Alice wasn't making it interesting enough?

Alice jumped up and went back to her desk and pulled out a hot-pink Post-it note from her Post-it note holder (completely unnecessary but she loved the way it always helpfully spat out a single stickie). She began to brainstorm notebook topics that could guarantee a lengthy response from Cassidy.

Nikki Wilcox
Cute boy Jesse
Cafeteria food rankings
New lotion/perfume/nail polish reviews
TV show recaps

Predictions of who will take who to the snowball dance

Ms. Haynes's outfits???

Alice pondered and tapped the metal part of her pencil against her teeth until she got a headache.

"Alice, pizza!" her dad called, rescuing her from her self-imposed homework assignment. While getting her homework done this school year was going to be a challenge, keeping the notebook—which was basically a symbol of her and Cassidy's friendship—thriving was also going to take some effort. But Alice knew it would be worth it.

CHAPTER 5

FRIENDSHIP VS. HOMEWORK

"What would you guys most want to take with you if you were stranded on an island?" Mr. Nichols asked the class on Monday, leaning against the board, tossing a tiny nub of chalk up in the air and catching it. The class, still rusty from the weekend, looked blankly at him. "Well, don't all speak up at once. Come on. Alice, how about you?"

"Um, a tent?" Alice asked. *Pitiful.* She could be more creative than that.

"Okay," Mr. Nichols said. "Christy, how about you?"

"My dog!" she chirped. "He could keep me warm and provide company and maybe catch some food."

"All right," he said. "Companionship. Aaron, go."

"Um, my TV and the NFL package?" Aaron said.

"The joke answer—finally, somebody got it out of the way," Mr. Nichols said, tossing the piece of chalk gently at Aaron's forehead. Aaron caught the chalk and grinned. A few other kids burst forth with similarly goofy answers, realizing that it was safe to do so, with answers like "A smartphone!" or "A microwave!" or "A helicopter!"

"Okay, good. Let's keep this discussion in mind as we read our next book," Mr. Nichols said. "Because it may make you contemplate what's really important when you're on your own. I bring you . . . *Island of the Blue Dolphins*!" He passed out copies of the book, which featured a drawing of a small figure of a girl, standing alone on top of a cliff with her long dark hair blowing in the wind, dolphins swimming in the sea beneath her.

"This looks like a *girls'* book," Todd Tian complained. A couple of the guys around him snorted.

"And why do you say that, Mr. Tian?" Mr. Nichols inquired.

"It has a girl on the cover, is all," said Todd.

"That's it?" said Mr. Nichols.

"And, I don't know. Dolphins," said Todd, shrugging. "It just seems girly."

"Okay," said Mr. Nichols. "Did anybody else in here have the same reaction as Todd?" A few reluctant hands went up around the room.

"I want you all to put your books on the floor," Mr. Nichols said. "Quickly." An echo of *thwap*s went around the room as students dropped the paperbacks on the linoleum tile.

"Okay," said Mr. Nichols, writing two headings on the blackboard, one titled *GIRLS* and the other *BOYS*. "Quick, don't overthink it. What are some words you'd expect to read in the description of a girls' book?"

"Gossip!" said one girl.

"Friends!" shouted out another.

"Clothes!" came out another cry. Mr. Nichols wrote this all on the board.

"Mr. Nichols?" Alice raised her hand. He nodded at her.

"Um, wasn't *To Kill a Mockingbird* also about a girl, though?" she asked. "So did that make it a girls' book?"

Mr. Nichols pursed his lips and raised his eyebrows. "Yes, now that you mention it, it *was*, wasn't it?" he said. Alice felt a warm sensation and tried not to smile. English was by far her favorite class: they had cool conversations and Mr. Nichols actually seemed to want to listen to what the class thought. "Did you guys recall seeing a lot of gossip, friends, and clothes in that book?"

"Well," said Aaron hesitantly. "That book was *about* a girl but it wasn't, like, a girls' book."

"So who was it for, then?" said Mr. Nichols.

"Uh, everybody?" Aaron said, shrinking down in his

chair and looking off to the side like he didn't want to be there anymore.

"Okay," said Mr. Nichols. "I'll quit torturing you guys soon, I promise. But, what are some words you would associate with what you'd call a boys' book?"

Nobody raised his or her hand. Mr. Nichols looked around. "Nikki Wilcox, you've been awfully quiet," he said.

Nikki rolled her dark eyes and pushed up the sleeves of her long-sleeved white T-shirt. "Nobody wants to say anything because they realize already that, like, the whole boys' books versus girls' books concept is dumb," she said. "We wouldn't be having this conversation if Todd had just kept his mouth shut." Todd glowered at his hands.

Harsh but true, Alice thought. The room felt awkward, but Alice was invigorated by the discussion. Mr. Nichols was treating them like grown-ups and actually getting them to think and talk about books instead of just making them read for no particular reason. Finally it actually felt like honors classes were paying off.

"People should feel free to say what they think in this class—within reason," said Mr. Nichols. "But listen, I promise I won't judge any of you, and neither will your classmates. I'm actually trying to get at something here,

I swear. Boys' books. Go."

The students threw out words like "fight" and "sports" and "adventure," which Mr. Nichols added to the board.

"Good," he said. "Okay, you may rescue your books from the floor. You can apologize to them too, if you are sorry for mistreating them."

"I'm sorry, book!" Todd clowned around, holding his book up in the air and gazing at it. "I will never do that to you again!" The students laughed.

"Okay, Todd," Mr. Nichols said. "The spotlight is yours, since you seem to need it so badly today. Do me a favor and read the description of *Island of the Blue Dolphins* on the back aloud to the class."

Todd turned his book over in his hands and cleared his throat dramatically. "The story of a twelve-year-old girl who lives alone on a Pacific island after she leaps from a rescue ship. Isolated on the island for eighteen years, Karana forages for food, builds weapons to fight predators, clothes herself in a cormorant-feathered skirt, and finds strength and peace in her seclusion."

"All right," said Mr. Nichols. "Very nice, Todd. So what do you guys notice?"

"Well, it *does* have the word 'clothes' in it," pointed out Aaron.

"'Fight' and 'weapons' and 'predators'" are in there too," offered Christy, twirling her wooden cuff bracelet around her wrist. "So she's a tough girl."

"Righto," said Mr. Nichols. "So what do you guys think I'm getting at here?" he said.

"That Todd needs to stop talking!" offered Ashley Dawson in the back. Everyone laughed uproariously; studious Ashley rarely spoke in class, which made her takedown even funnier.

"I think you want us not to judge a book by its cover," said Alice.

"And that maybe just because a book is *about a girl* doesn't mean it's a book *for* girls," added Aaron.

"That's right," said Mr. Nichols. "I know I'm old and everything, but I hope you trust me when it comes to what I choose for you to read. It wouldn't make for a very interesting class if half of you were completely tuned out when it came to our discussions and homework."

Mr. Nichols glanced at the clock on the wall that, for some reason, was protected by a metal cage, as if people were constantly throwing rocks at it. "Good talk today, guys. And with that, it looks like our time is almost up for the day, so I would like to thank you all for such a spirited discussion." The class beamed at the compliment. "But you're not off the hook. Have the first three chapters of the book read by tomorrow," Mr. Nichols said, to a chorus of class groaning. "And be ready to discuss. Clearly you all have opinions and have no problem expressing them, so I expect a lot more good feedback tomorrow."

The bell rang and the students stood up, gathering their things to head to the next class. Alice could tell that everyone else—like her—felt inspired by the discussion. She even felt a little more mature, and possibly like she had grown an extra half inch taller, if that were possible.

"I kind of love this class, don't you?" she asked over her shoulder to someone she thought was Ashley Dawson, who wore her long, straight dark hair down today, along with a cute black-and-white dress. But Alice did a double take—it wasn't Ashley she was talking to, it was Nikki, who, with her dark curly hair, white tee, and black skirt, looked like Ashley in Alice's periphery.

For a second, Nikki looked like she was going to respond like a normal human being—but then a hard look fell over Nikki's face. She narrowed her eyes and stomped around her to get to biology. *Yeesh*, Alice thought. *I was just trying to be positive about class. I wonder what her problem is.*

"That was kind of fun, huh?" said Aaron, shouldering his blue backpack as they trekked across the hall to the lab.

"Yeah!" Alice said, relieved that she wasn't the only one who liked Mr. Nichols. The honors class was quickly becoming its own group of friends—aside from Nikki. There was a sort of chicken-and-egg situation with Nikki, Alice realized. Was she separate from the class because she was so negative and hard to include, or did she just want to do her own thing, apart from everybody else, and that was why she *seemed* so cranky? *Either way, it's like she's making it hard for herself on purpose. Why would she do that?* Alice pondered, then shook her head, as if to get Nikki's grumpy dust off her. *It's not my problem!*

Alice was en route to Ms. Crawford's class when she saw Cassidy emerge from her math class. Cassidy didn't see Alice at first, and Alice was able to observe, from a slight distance, how happy and popular Cassidy looked. She wore a bright red dress with black high-tops, and her hair was growing out into a petite Afro, which she wore like a crown. Xia, April, and Evie (who had cut her hair short recently too, although she swore it wasn't because she was copying Cassidy) hovered around her as they laughed at some joke Cassidy had made.

Look, she doesn't need you, a tiny voice in Alice's head whispered.

Oh, shut up! Alice thought in response. She marched up to Cassidy and whispered breathlessly in her ear, "Oh my goodness, can we *please* have an emergency hangout tonight? I need to tell you about the weirdest encounter I just had with Nikki Wilcox."

"What? Oh, totally," said Cassidy. "I *need* to hear this. Come to my place after school?" Alice nodded, squeezed into biology just as the bell was ringing, and slid into her desk right on time. She glanced over at Nikki, who seemed to be reading her textbook—three chapters ahead. What a weirdo. It was like she went out of her way not to have any friends. Alice wondered what Nikki would be like if she had a best friend, a Cassidy in her life. But that would mean Nikki had actually bothered to talk to someone else for once. Maybe even smile at them!

Alice pulled the purple notebook out of her bag to write down what had just happened.

Have you learned anything more about why Nikki Wilcox is the way she is? Is her mother a rhino and her father a crab?

Alice decided to go ahead and write a good lengthy entry about the last few days. Maybe she'd encourage Cassidy to write something nice and long too.

You know how we played all that badminton in your backyard last summer and got really good at it? Well, in gym class yesterday this guy from the intramural soccer team went around challenging everyone, and I totally beat him! I wish you had been there to see it.

Alice glanced up to make sure that she still was engaged with the class. Ms. Crawford was going over photosynthesis, which Alice had learned all about last year, when she'd coaxed a plant to grow through a maze she'd created out of cardboard boxes, in order to reach a sun lamp she'd placed at the other end. She kept the plant with its heart-shaped leaves on her desk at home, where it grew and grew like a girl's hair, eventually reaching the floor. Last year for Valentine's Day, she had given Cassidy a few clippings of the plant in a small pink pot, and it made Alice happy to see it growing every time she went to the Turners'.

Alice, stumped for additional funny stories, glanced

over at Nikki, who sat at the lab table a few people down from her, jotting notes furiously on a legal pad while Ms. Crawford spoke. Alice noticed that in profile, as she concentrated, Nikki's pouting lips made a perfect heart shape, just like Alice's and Nikki's plants. But suddenly Nikki's face transformed into a snarl as she hissed at Aaron Woolsey, who was sitting next to her, "Would you stop that? It's really annoying!" Aaron had been absentmindedly tapping his pen against the edge of the tabletop while Ms. Crawford spoke.

"Sorry," whispered Aaron, looking a little hurt and pointedly laying the pen on top of the lab table. Even Ms. Crawford briefly paused during her lecture but decided to keep going once she realized nothing dramatic was happening. Alice's heart broke a little bit. Aaron was so nice to *everyone*—she couldn't believe that Nikki had just been mean to him!

YOU WOULD NOT BELIEVE HOW MEAN NEGATIVE NIKKI JUST WAS—AND THIS IS THE THIRD TIME TODAY.

Maybe Cassidy had learned something in ballet or from one of Nikki's former elementary school classmates about why she was the way she was.

Oh no. Alice realized, with a pang of disappointment, that she couldn't, shouldn't, go to Cassidy's tonight—she had to read *Island of the Blue Dolphins* instead. Since she'd never read it before, she had to pay much closer attention than she had to with *To Kill a Mockingbird*, plus she had homework from math and probably would from biology too.

It would be smarter to stay home and get her work done, but the idea of not seeing her best friend was just too much, especially after a day like today.

You can get the reading done, Alice told herself. *You made it through last week, right?*

Alice alternated between fretting over what was the right choice and halfheartedly jotting down some notes from class so she could do the homework exercise later.

The bell, signaling lunch, momentarily saved her from her wishy-washiness. But by the time Alice had gathered her things, smoothed down the skirt of her royal-blue dress, and gotten to the door, she could only just see the top of Cassidy's head as she and her friends sauntered down the hall to the cafeteria.

Alice made a decision: *I'm going to Cassidy's house. I'll get my homework done . . . eventually.* She picked her chin up and tried to do an impression of a confident person, one who had time for both homework and friends. *At least I don't look like* her, Alice thought as she watched Nikki make a beeline for the door after class, her eyes staring at the ground.

CHAPTER 6

NEGATIVE NIKKI DEBRIEF

I needed this, Alice told herself, feeling the instant relaxation that came over her whenever she went over to Cassidy's house. She let herself sink in a little deeper into the soft, creamy white leather couch and took a moment to inhale—*aaah.*

Mrs. Turner was obsessed with good smells, and so each room in the house was a little treat for the nose. Depending on what Cassidy's mom was in the mood for, some days the kitchen smelled like apples (others vanilla), the powder room like fall potpourri (others baby powder), the living room like roses (others white musk), and Cassidy's room like lavender (other days patchouli), thanks to the candles, incense, and essential oils that Mrs. Turner tucked into the corners of the house. Alice wished her mom would embrace Mrs. Turner's philosophy of "Decorating with scent!" but the one time Mrs. Turner sent Alice home with a cone of incense she had complimented (something that smelled ancient and spicy, like the inside of an old church), Mrs. Kinney had freaked.

"Is that *smoke*?" she had asked, seeing the tiny pillar of white emanating from Alice's desk.

"It's just incense, Mom," Alice explained.

"Alice, you could burn the house down," Mrs. Kinney said, and before Alice could protest, Mrs. Kinney grabbed Alice's glass of water and swept the innocent little cone into the water with Alice's ruler, creating a *hiss* sound and a dark cloud in the glass.

"*Mom*," Alice had said.

"I'll get you a new water," Mrs. Kinney said. "And no candles or incense or whatever this is until you get your *own* house. And even then I think it's a bad idea." Alice made do with some essential oil sticks she kept on her vanity stand, but it just wasn't the same without that quiet little plume of smoke keeping her company.

"Want to go upstairs?" Cassidy asked, walking out of the kitchen. "I've got refreshments," she said, and waved around two yellow-and-blue plates laden with slices of Mrs. Turner's killer chocolate cheesecake.

"This is *so* much better than doing homework!" Alice said as they climbed the stairs to Cassidy's room. The wooden stairs were lined with a thick red carpet that ran down the center, so Alice felt like a celebrity whenever they went upstairs.

"I can't believe how much homework you guys get," Cassidy said as they entered her room. It was painted a deep midnight purple and decorated with huge black-and-white photos of Cassidy dancing, twirling and jumping and bowing confidently, like a queen accepting a crown. Alice wished her room looked as sophisticated as her best friend's. They arranged themselves on the black-and-white carpeted floor, propped up by huge teal throw pillows

"What's up, Dingae?" called a voice from Cassidy's door. Alice looked up to see David, Cassidy's older brother, a tall and confident eighth grader with beautiful straight teeth newly revealed after a long and awkward bout with braces.

When they were little and would fight, David would call Cassidy a dingus, but when Alice was over and the two would play pranks on him during sleepovers (mostly dumb stuff like taping down the light switch in his bedroom or writing notes on the toilet paper in his bathroom), he'd refer to them as Dingus One (Cassidy) and Dingus Two (Alice), and he had decided that together they were Dingae. They hadn't played pranks on David in a long time, but he still used the nicknames, which Alice secretly loved.

As an only child, Alice yearned to have someone in the house to talk to who wasn't her parents. Cassidy reassured her that having a big brother wasn't *all* that, but still, Alice suspected it was still pretty fun to have someone else around.

"We're just catching up on the day," Cassidy said, holding her plate out of harm's way as David inched towards her with one finger out, pretending he was going to dig into her cake. "We have a rude-girl situation on our hands."

"Rude-girl situation?" David asked. "You mean aside from the one I see right here?" He pointed at Cassidy.

"Oh, get out," Cassidy said. "Don't you have some eighth-grade business to attend to?"

"Ah, yes," David said. "Important matters. Top secret. I can't tell you about it. You may understand . . . some day. See ya, Number One and Number Two."

"He's such a turd." Cassidy sighed, settling into her pillows. She arranged her long legs, clad in leggings spotted with gold studs, in front of her and took a dainty bite of her cheesecake. Licking her fingers, she perused the notebook, which Alice had placed on the floor between them, raising her head and making comments about Alice's stories.

"Aaron really seems like a sweetie. We should see if he wants to go to the movies with you and me and Jesse sometime!" and "Did you see that necklace with the bow on it Christy was wearing the other day? I wanted it so bad!" Then she got to the most recent entry, with Alice's huge furious, angry writing about Nikki.

"Whoa," Cassidy said. "Nobody makes my best friend mad like this! Let's talk." She set down her plate in a let's-get-serious way, but before they could talk, the girls were interrupted by a tan-and-black blur that tore into the bedroom, yipping and snorting. It was Bagel, Cassidy's pet pug, who David must have let inside without giving any warning.

"No, Bagel, no!" Cassidy laughed as her dog tried frantically to eat the rest of her cheesecake. "Oh my goodness, he is such a little demon. But how could you not love a face like this?" she said, finally catching Bagel and holding his head still in her hand. Alice smiled politely. Just being around Bagel made her break out into hives, start sneezing, and get watery eyes. But on top of that, she secretly didn't think Bagel was so cute. His eyes were all bloodshot and bugged out of his head, and his face looked like a soda-pop can somebody had stepped on. His little butt had weird little patterns on it. Plus, he barked. All the time. Loudly.

"Oh well," Cassidy said. "Out you go."

To Alice's relief, Cassidy escorted Bagel outside and shut the door.

"This house is so ridiculous," Cassidy said. "Too many distractions!" Bagel scratched and whined at the door, begging to be let in. "Bagel's like, 'Are you *sure* you're allergic? Can you check again to see if we can have some fun?'"

"Sorry, Bagel!" Alice called at the door, and Bagel let out a little wet-sounding huffy growl. The girls laughed.

"Okay," said Cassidy, once they could concentrate. "Finally. Tell me everything that happened today with Nikki." So Alice went back over the day's events, from Nikki basically saying everyone was dumb during English, to her cold shoulder after class, to her shutting down Aaron Woolsey during biology.

One of the things Alice loved most about Cassidy was that she was such a great listener. The time Alice had informed Cassidy that her parents were taking her on a totally boring Civil War battle-site road tour during what was supposed to be a perfectly normal summer, she had widened her eyes so huge in disbelief that Alice could see the whites all around. She asked, "Are you being punished for something?" And Alice immediately cracked up. Cassidy always knew how to make Alice laugh about something that seemed terrible at first.

The day that Alice complained to Cassidy that Mrs. Koshy was making her run laps in gym class for not showing enough "hustle," Cassidy shook her head like she was a tired old woman and replied, "Mrs. Koshy wouldn't know hustle if it kicked her in the booty."

When Alice and Cassidy did their post-Christmas rundown last year and Alice moaned about her aunt serving fruitcake and *nothing else* for dessert, Cassidy pursed her lips and grunted in disapproval (before sending Alice home with some leftover Christmas cookies from her family holiday).

She always made Alice feel like she was telling a really interesting story, instead of just griping about some girl in class. This particular time, with each story about Nikki's mean comments, cold shoulders, and dark looks, Cassidy widened her eyes twice, shook her head once, grunted twice, and finished with an "Oh no she didn't!"

"I can't believe she was so mean to you, not to mention that nice boy of yours," Cassidy said. She was determined to get Alice and Aaron together, even though Alice had told her a million times it would never happen—this year, anyway.

"Well, he's not mine, remember," Alice said. "But

yes. You should have seen his face, Cassidy—she was so mean!"

"You need to steer clear of that girl," Cassidy said. "Don't talk to her—don't even look at her again. She's bad news."

"I know," said Alice, who was doing her best to carve her last bite of cheesecake into a thousand tiny bites in order to make it last.

"No, seriously, she's totally stuck-up," Cassidy said. "In ballet on Monday we were working on this one routine, where you have to go like this—" Cassidy jumped up and demonstrated six or seven tiny precise moves.

"So it's pretty complicated, right?" said Cassidy. "On my second try, instead of going like *this*"—she crossed her ankles a particular way—"I went like *this*," she said, doing what seemed to Alice like exactly the same move, but apparently wasn't.

"I mean, it was just practice, right?" said Cassidy. "But instead that girl Nikki says, 'You're not supposed to do it like that! You're messing everything up! Blah blah blah!'" Cassidy stood with her heels together, rolling her eyes and using her hand as a puppet to imitate Nikki.

"That's awful," Alice said. "Why couldn't she just say something to you quietly?"

"Or just let it go?" Cassidy said. "She's not Madame Bernard. She's not the teacher. She's not my mom. She's not the boss of me! I don't need her to tell me what I'm doing wrong. Especially not in front of everyone!"

"Maybe she wants to be a teacher someday," Alice reasoned. "A mean one, like Ms. Garrity."

"It was totally embarrassing," Cassidy said. "Everyone was looking at me. And Madame Bernard was like, 'Thank you, Nikki, for your gentle guidance,' and Nikki smiled, but I think Madame Bernard was sort of hinting to her not to be such a know-it-all.

"*And,*" Cassidy said, "that's not even the end of it. She *still* is too good to hang out with us after class. I even made a point of asking her, 'Nikki, do you want some pretzels and hummus?' but she just looked at me and said, 'I have to go,' and left. No 'thank you' or anything."

"Would you even want to hang out with her after class?" Alice wondered. "Since she's so mean?"

Cassidy snorted. "Definitely not. But you'd think that maybe she could take five minutes to say, 'Hey, Cassidy, sorry I was totally rude to you during class, I'm just having a bad day,' or something like that. It's like she totally hates being in class with all of us."

"She seems so mad about everything," Alice agreed.

"Maybe her brain is full of bugs," Cassidy said. "Like, maybe a really angry spider crawled into her ear while she was sleeping one night and it laid eggs and now a hundred angry baby spiders are running around in there. And they're not just angry, they're pooping."

"Oh my god!" Alice said, covering her eyes and laughing. "Cassidy, that's so gross."

"The spider is gonna get ya!" Cassidy said, creeping towards Alice with a single finger stretched out. She poked Alice in the stomach, making her shriek. The girls laughed uproariously, making Bagel go nuts outside Cassidy's door, running around and yipping louder. Alice would never understand dogs.

"Oh, Nikki," Cassidy said. "Why do you have to bring us all down?"

"Ah, let's not talk about her anymore," Alice said. She felt so good right now. She had made the right choice to come over to Cassidy's. *I'll get my work done later,* she promised herself, and then instantly regretted even thinking about her homework, because it brought her happiness down just a few notches.

"Hey," said Alice, nodding over at the flip camera resting on Cassidy's desk. "Let's make a movie."

"Oh my god, we haven't done that in *so long!*" Cassidy said, jumping to her feet to grab the camera.

The girls spent nearly an hour narrating sketches they made up about the silly photos in fashion magazines.

"Hey, Susie, what on earth are you wearing?" Alice asked a photo of a model who was proudly strutting around in flowy floral pants under a white crocheted vest. It might have been fashionable somewhere else, like *Mars*, but it would never fly on the North Shore.

"I got it from my grandma!" Cassidy narrated on behalf of the model. "She's the coolest girl I know. She's eighty years old and her name is Agnes and sometimes when we're feeling feisty we eat mashed-up bananas together!" Alice put her hand over her mouth so she wouldn't laugh out loud during the take.

"What's going on with you, Petunia Poutyface?" Cassidy asked a model who looked out of the page sadly, wearing a cropped blue leather shirt and crunchy, side-swept hair, and sat on the floor with her feet twisted towards each other.

"I was so busy doing my hair today that I forgot how to walk!" said Cassidy in a baby voice.

"Um, also, where are your pants?" asked Alice.

"Silly girl, everyone knows that not wearing pants is the new pants!" said Cassidy.

"Looking ridiculous is the new looking awesome!" added Alice.

Mrs. Turner knocked softly on Cassidy's door and opened it. "Alice, honey? Your mom just called. She says it's time for dinner."

"Ah, man!" said Cassidy. "Can't Alice stay for dinner?"

"She's always welcome, but not when her mom has cooked dinner for her already," said Mrs. Turner. "And I heard it's lasagna night too," she said, knowing Alice's favorite.

"All right," said Alice, scrambling to her feet. "I guess I better go."

"Okay, well, listen." Cassidy stood up and drew an invisible box around Alice. "This is your force field. Don't let Negative Nikki enter it. If you stay inside your force field, you're golden," Cassidy said. "I'll see you tomorrow!"

"Don't forget to write!" Alice said, heading out the door, pointing at the notebook. Cassidy blew her a kiss.

Sometimes Alice wished the walk home to her house was slightly longer than just across the street. The air smelled like a wood-burning fire, and the setting sun was throwing gorgeous purple and orange light behind the clouds. It had turned out to be a great day. And now Alice got to eat lasagna!

"How was your day?" Alice's dad asked as the family sat down to a big, crunchy first-course salad. Alice tucked one leg beneath her at the table and excitedly told them all about the cool discussion they had had in Mr. Nichols's class and how much fun she had with Cassidy.

"That sounds great!" said Mr. Kinney. "Do I dare say that you had fun and were learning at the same time?"

"Maybe!" said Alice.

"And you start reading *Island of the Blue Dolphins* tonight?" Mrs. Kinney asked. She had little ways of checking in on Alice's homework without actually standing over her daughter's shoulder.

Normally Alice didn't mind a question like this, but she instantly grew irritated. Her mom just *had* to remind her about her homework, bringing her down from her best friend-and-lasagna high.

"Yes, I'll start reading the book," Alice said testily. "After I have dinner. Is that all right with you?" Her red hair slipped from behind her ears, forming a curtain around her face. She felt like Nikki, who always seemed to use her dark hair like a wall.

"Uh, yes, Ms. Touchy," her dad said, eyeing her. "Take it down a notch. Your mom was just asking."

"As long as I know you're working and parent-teacher conferences are pleasant, I can sleep at night," her mom said.

"Sorry," Alice apologized. While she had had so much fun with Cassidy, she also knew that she should have gotten a jump on her homework already. Mr. Nichols expected a lot of input from the class on *Dolphins* after their discussion earlier today. She swallowed some milk to wash down her lasagna. "May I be excused? I guess I might as well get to work."

"I'll save you some leftovers for later," her mom promised as Alice grabbed her backpack and headed up to her room. *I just need to focus up and get everything done and everything will work out,* she told herself. She pulled the tall chair up to the drafting table and got to work.

After breezing through her math homework and polishing up her report on DNA for biology, Alice sat at her desk and cracked open *Island of the Blue Dolphins*. It was fine, but just a few pages in, she realized that the fall evening had cast a chill over the house, and she'd be much more comfortable under the covers in bed. And if she *were* under the covers in bed, all snuggly and warm, wouldn't it be a shame to have to get up and get *out* of bed in order to get ready for bed?

So, even though it was early, Alice put on her cuddliest pair of pajamas (flannel, decorated with cute drawings of purple wiener dogs on them), brushed her teeth, washed her face, and said good night to her parents, who distractedly said good night back. They were lost in an epic Scrabble battle against each other in the living room (whoever won had to make—*and* clean up—dinner the next day).

Finally Alice climbed into bed with the book, feeling comfy and cozy. But just another few pages in, and she felt her eyelids getting heavy.

No! she told herself, and sat up, pulling her white fluffy comforter down so that she wouldn't feel too likely to fall asleep. *Finish the chapter at least!* But her mom's lasagna and Mrs. Turner's cheesecake lingered in her tummy, making her feel content and sleepy and full.

You shouldn't have gone over to Cassidy's! an annoying voice in her head told her.

Well, it's too late to think about that now, she reasoned. *Plus, all work and no play is no good for anybody, right?* She read a few more pages before starting to feel sleepy again. Alice contemplated sitting on the floor in order to get up to page thirty-five, the way she was supposed to. *But it's so nice and warm in bed!* one of the annoying voices argued, but the voice slowly turned into a whisper. Alice drifted off to sleep, her book open to page eleven on her chest.

CHAPTER 7

NERD HERD RISING

"*That's* an interesting look!" Alice was so busy trying to cram in the last several pages of her *Island of the Blue Dolphins* reading assignment that she didn't even see Cassidy sidle up next to her at the bus stop. She looked adorable as usual, in a black kilt with a white dress shirt that looked like she had borrowed from David and a cheetah-print T-shirt layered over that. Alice, meanwhile, was wearing navy sweatpants, a soft-gray T-shirt, a long purple cardigan, and gym shoes.

"Ugh," she said, putting a finger in her book for a moment. "I fell asleep last night before I could finish my homework, and I'm trying to use every spare second I have to finish up," she explained. "So this was the first thing I could grab to wear without having to think."

"That stinks," Cassidy said. "I mean about the homework, not your 'outfit,'" she explained, grinning and making quotation marks with her fingers. Alice stuck her tongue out at her. "No, seriously, you look fine. Comfy chic. But do you want me to leave you alone so you can read? I can write funny encouraging things in the notebook while we wait."

"Yeah, sorry," Alice said, picking her book back up. She hated to turn down quality time with Cassidy, but if she didn't get to work, she'd fall behind and be the victim of one of Mr. Nichols's pop quizzes he was always threatening. So far they had been safe, but Alice didn't want to find out today if he was just bluffing. She read as fast as she could, feeling better as she spied Cassidy scribbling away in the notebook out of the corner of her eye. *Island of the Blue Dolphins* was fine, but one of Cassidy's entries would be infinitely more fun to read—a treat for getting through the homework.

After the bus arrived, Alice huddled over her paperback on the window side of the bus bench. Cassie leaned over and chatted with Tess Sawyer about some posters that had gone up the day before, advertising the school musical.

"Do you think they'd let us audition?" asked Cassidy.

"I don't see why not," said Tess. "I didn't read anything on the poster about auditions being limited to any particular classes. Do you think you'll try out?"

"Oh, *maybe*," Cassidy said in a coy voice. "I don't like attention that much."

"Girl, please!" Tess said. "Were you or were you not the girl singing 'Let It Go' in the locker room at the top of your voice yesterday after gym?"

"I can't help it if it's got great acoustics!" Cassidy said, and she and Tess laughed. Alice, meanwhile, tried to keep her ears shut and her mind on her reading.

"All done?" Cassidy asked as they exited the bus once they got to school. Alice had temporarily put the book away so she wouldn't trip on the way in, although falling on her face and going to the nurse's *would* be a good way to avoid a pop quiz.

"Almost there," Alice said. "I'll get the rest done in homeroom."

"Okay, well, take this for when you're done," Cassidy said, slipping the notebook into Alice's backpack. "I'll see you at lunch. Good luck!" Alice flashed a grateful smile to Cassidy, whose big brown eyes were warm and understanding.

Just five pages to go, Alice told herself once she got to homeroom, but as the class filled up, she had a hard time concentrating. It was like everyone in the class had taken energy pills, aside from Alice (and of course Nikki, who was gloomily examining her hair for split ends).

"Guys, I've decided we need to come up with a name for ourselves," Christy Gillespie announced to the room before the bell rang. "My sister and I got into a fight last night because she said that I'm on dork patrol. I think she was just jealous because my parents like that I'm in honors. But it got me thinking . . . why not have a name for ourselves, like we're a team? Like Geek Squad or something."

"I don't think we're geeks," said Aaron Woolsey thoughtfully. "Geeks make me think of people who wear glasses. And none of us wear glasses, except for Todd." Todd proudly took off his specs, breathed on them, and polished them with a corner of his plaid shirt.

"The Brainy Bunch?" suggested Ashley Dawson.

"That's the way we became the Brainy Bunch!" a few of the girls sang to the tune of *The Brady Bunch* theme song before laughing.

The class went back and forth until Alice couldn't take it anymore. The answer was so obvious. She put her book pages-down on her desk and said, "Guys. We're the Nerd Herd."

"Nerd Herd!" Christy clapped her hands with glee. "That's it!"

"You did it again, Kinney." Aaron extended his palm for a high five. He began a chant. "Nerd Herd! Nerd

Herd! Nerd Herd!" Everyone in the room gathered steam as Alice tried not to blush. It was so silly, but she had to admit she was having fun. The only person who seemed like she wasn't in on it, of course, was Nikki, whose nose was now deep in her math textbook. She was acting like she was wearing invisible earplugs.

"All right, simmer," said Ms. Garrity, allowing herself to crack a small smile as she entered the room.

Alice had a few short minutes to spare before the bell rang, and so she scanned, as quickly as she could, the last few pages of the last chapter of the reading assignment. She sent up a quick prayer that this wouldn't be the day that Mr. Nichols decided to quiz them all on the assignment. She hid a yawn behind her fist: not only was she *not* totally one hundred percent sure what she was reading, but she was exhausted too from all the morning cramming.

After homeroom wrapped up (Ms. Garrity confirmed that, indeed, the school musical was coming and that students were encouraged to try out), Alice lingered a second to write a quick note to Cassidy. She opened it up and was touched to see an encouraging collage Cassidy had put together the night before. She had cut out words like "inspiration" and "determination" from some magazines, along with a photo of a cute boy giving the thumbs-up sign and a picture of a sandwich in a panini press (which Cassidy had explained by writing next to it, "I know you're going to *crush* your class today! Get it? Let me know if you don't.")

The only way it could have meant more to Alice was if it had summed up the reading from the night before. Alice decided to take a quick second and write a reply back to Cassidy before class.

Thanks for the note! Here's hoping I don't totally flunk the quiz, or, even better, that there is no quiz. I think I got the reading done okay, but we were pretty distracted in homeroom deciding that we're going to call ourselves the Nerd Herd. I mean, how cheesy is that? But it's fun. Of course you can guess who <u>did not</u> want to have anything to do with it. She who must not be named. (Her name is Nikki, in case you couldn't guess!) It's not like we're excluding her. It's like she'd rather be anywhere else! It must be exactly like what goes on after ballet. Okay, I gotta jam across the hall. Nerd Herd out.

Alice got up and tucked the notebook next to her copy of *Dolphins* in her panda bag. *Oh well*, Alice thought. *Here goes nothing.*

Both the good news and bad news seemed to be that Alice wasn't the only one who hadn't quite gotten the reading done for Mr. Nichols's class. After the promising discussion the day before, the students were quiet and unwilling to talk.

"So what do you guys think so far?" he asked, walking around to the windows and spraying one of the many plants in his classroom with a mister.

Silence.

"How does it compare to the first couple of chapters of *To Kill a Mockingbird*?"

More silence.

"Hello?" Mr. Nichols said, spritzing the back of Aaron's neck a little bit. "Are you guys there?"

Aaron smiled and wiped the back of his neck off. "It's fine. I don't know, I'm still getting into it. It's just . . . *different.*"

"Anything else?" Mr. Nichols asked to the still-silent room. He might as well have been asking his plants. "I'm going to start calling on you guys if you don't start answering questions," Mr. Nichols warned.

More silence.

Alice stared down at her nails, which she had painted green with blue tips during one of her hangout sessions with Cassidy. The blue was starting to chip away. *Please, oh please,* Alice issued forth a silent wish. *Not me.*

"So what did you guys think about Karana's father advising everyone to avoid making friends with the Aleuts?" Mr. Nichols asked the group. "I want to hear from . . . Alice." His name fell on her head like a ton of bricks. *Arg.*

"Um," Alice said. "Well." She *knew* what Mr. Nichols was talking about. Her brain just seemed much more disorganized than usual, though. So much for sounding somewhat intelligent today.

"What kind of mentality does it create?" He tried rephrasing.

Alice silently scolded herself for reading so fast and not taking her time the way she usually did. Usually when she read for class she circled words that stood out to her, wrote notes in the margins, dog-eared pages that looked important. Now, in her mind's eye, the pages of the reading chapters flew by, the words a blur.

"It creates an us-versus-them mentality.'" Alice heard a know-it-all voice over her shoulder. She looked behind her, even though it was obvious who was talking. "It means that Karana is being encouraged to look at the Aleuts not as individuals but as a group. A *herd*." Nikki sneered. "I mean, it's obvious if you did the reading."

"I did the reading," Alice said defensively. Nikki rolled her eyes.

"Okay then," said Mr. Nichols, looking confused, like *Something is going on here, and I don't know what it is, but I don't like it.* "Thanks, Nikki. Let's move on."

"I wish somebody would leave *you* on an island," Alice heard someone mutter. Todd Tian was looking sideways at Nikki, and everyone who heard snickered quietly. He was still mad, it seemed, about Nikki calling him out during the *To Kill a Mockingbird* discussion.

Alice felt a little proud that Todd had stuck up for her. The class was becoming a team after all, but when she snuck a look at Nikki, she saw her skin turning the same shade of pink as her hoodie, which was a deep blush. She felt a little bit bad for Nikki—until Nikki looked up, saw Alice glancing at her, and gave the most evil, narrow-eyed, force-field-penetrating look she'd ever seen in her life. *Yikes!*

Mr. Nichols eventually gave up and made the last fifteen minutes of class quiet reading time.

Phew, Alice wrote to Cassidy.

We didn't get quizzed, but I sure did fall on my face and look dumb in front of everyone. Can you guess who helped make me feel real good about it too?

In the cafeteria, where the chattering echoed off the ugly red-tiled floor and onto the even uglier white-tiled ceiling, it looked like the Nerd Herd was continuing the togetherness outside the classroom. Alice smiled and waved at a table where Aaron, Todd, Ashley, and even shy Nisha Pakoor were all sitting together. She would have taken her tray over there too if Cassidy hadn't saved a seat for her with Xia, April, and Evie.

"Boy, have I got a Nikki Wilcox story for *you,*" Alice said with a sigh, setting down her tray with its uninspiring veggie burger, which she suspected was just made up of old paper from the recycling bin. She had been in such a rush that morning, she'd forgotten to take her leftover lasagna.

"Hold on a sec," Cassidy said. "Evie was just telling us about what her big sister had told her about the school musical."

Evie leaned over the table and ran the heart locket on her necklace up and down its chain, whispering like she was letting them in on some big secret. "So anyway,

Carrie said it's a ton of fun. Mr. Shankman, the director, lets everyone sort of take control and come up with ideas for the costumes and sets and everything. And there's a big cast party after the last show, which she said was one of the best nights she ever had in middle school." Evie's sister, Carrie, was in high school, and the girls were always hungry for any details of what middle school was like when she was younger—and what they had in store for them in high school.

"That sounds like so much fun," Cassidy said. "I've always wanted to do more singing, but for some reason Madame Bernard doesn't appreciate my talent!"

"Ms. Turner, now is not the time to sing, now is the time to dance!" Xia shouted in a high voice, apparently calling back something hilarious from dance class that Alice had missed out on.

"I was trying to sing 'Under the Sea' while we were doing this mermaid dance," Cassidy explained.

"Oh my gosh, guess what," Alice suddenly heard behind her. She turned to see Christy Gillespie from the Nerd Herd crouching down behind her chair, her perfectly shaped eyebrows arched high on her forehead.

"What's going on?" Alice asked, turning around and folding her arms over the plastic orange chair. The girls she was sitting with wouldn't mind that much if she turned her attention away for a second or two. She could hear them behind her, now trying to figure out if cool Ms. Haynes had a boyfriend or not.

"I just went to use the bathroom and walked by the courtyard," Christy said. "And who should I see out there, sitting by her lonesome, eating lunch solo beneath a sad little tree, but Nikki Wilcox!"

"Oh yeah," Alice said, scanning the noisy lunch-room. "I guess she isn't in here."

"And," Christy said breathlessly, bouncing on the balls of her feet, which were clad in blue leopard-print slip-on sneakers, "not only was she eating by herself, but she was reading *Island of the Blue Dolphins*. Like, I get it, we're the Nerd Herd, but it's okay to not study for *one second*!"

"Oh my goodness." Cassidy leaned over the table and joined in the conversation. "Does that girl have *any* friends?"

"*And* she's doing homework during lunch?" said Xia. "That means she's too nerdy even for the Nerd Herd!"

"Hey!" Christy said, raising a warning finger but smiling. "You know how it's okay if I talk smack about my mom but you're not allowed to? Only members of the Nerd Herd may make fun of Nerd Herders."

"I almost . . . *almost* . . . feel kind of bad for her," Alice admitted. It'd be one thing if Nikki was mean *and* popular, but she couldn't help wondering if Nikki would be different if she had some friends—or just one friend, even.

"Even after she was so nasty during class today?" Christy said.

Alice shrugged. "Maybe there's a reason why she's the way she is?"

"Well," Christy said. "I was talking to Aaron—they went to elementary school together but she didn't arrive until fourth grade. He said that she's always kept to herself, even after she'd been there for a whole year. It's like she doesn't want to make friends or something."

"That *is* kind of sad," admitted Cassidy. "Although I don't know if it's sad-sad or, like, pitiful-sad."

"I kinda think that if she's going to be rude, she gets what she deserves," said Christy. Alice shrugged. "But maybe you're right. You're a nicer person than I am, Alice." She grinned at Alice's table and skipped back to her seat. "See you, ladies!" Alice saw Aaron looking over at her table and offered him a wave. She sort of wished she was sitting over there, with the rest of the Herd, just to hear what they were talking about.

"Oh, you guys," Cassidy said. "I almost forgot to tell

you about this crazy old book of my mom's she showed me. It's called *Color Me Beautiful* and it says that each woman's complexion matches a season and she should dress like that season. Like I'm a winter and so I look good in, like, blue and silver and white."

"You look good in everything, girl!" said Xia.

"I mean, obviously," Cassidy said, holding up her hand like a pocket mirror and admiring herself in it. "Anyway, I want to bring it to lunch tomorrow because a) the outfits are hilarious—I mean, like, *skorts*, and also b) it could be fun to see what seasons we are. Alice, I'm thinking you're kind of a late summer. Evie, maybe for you, spring."

"Ooh, that's my favorite season!" squealed Evie.

The girls babbled about Cassidy's discovery, debating which seasons they would be and what colors they were destined to wear. Alice couldn't help but think about Nikki sitting out all by herself in the courtyard. Alice's friends and the Nerd Herd were both so easy to talk to and fun—why did Nikki separate herself?

Maybe Nikki had a reason for staying away. Maybe she was just smart about getting her work done. Alice had to admit to herself, *I should probably go out there and catch up on my reading too.*

Maybe Nikki's onto something.

CHAPTER 8

BEST FRIENDS SEPARATED

"We had such a fun discussion in class today," Alice bubbled to Cassidy on the bus ride home a few days later. After the first rough few days of *Dolphins*, the class had gotten back into the groove and discussion had picked up, and they finished the assignment without incident (or pop quiz). Mr. Nichols's class had been especially enjoyable lately, the Nerd Herd was gelling nicely, and for once, Nikki Wilcox seemed to be keeping her mean comments to herself. The sun was out and the air was crisp and cool—but not cold yet—and Alice felt invigorated.

"Hmm. 'Fun' and 'class' are not words that should go together," Cassidy joked. "Unless it's opposite day. Or I have been misled this entire time about what 'fun' actually is."

Alice smiled sympathetically. In Cassidy's latest

notebook entry, she had lamented that she wasn't doing so great in French class.

You know what would make French easier? If there were only one tense. Just live in the present! Viva la moment! Anyway, if I don't get my grades up my mom said she's going to make David start tutoring me, which makes me want to le vomit.

But Alice couldn't help herself. "Today we talked about what books we'd bury in a time capsule for future generations," she said.

"Aren't books just books?" Cassidy said. "Aren't they going to be there whether or not we'd put them in a time capsule? Isn't that what libraries are for?"

"No . . . you don't—" Alice was about to say, "You don't get it," but she caught herself. "The point was just to see what books we'd put in to illustrate what's important to us now."

"Oh," said Cassidy, looking out the window at the gray lake. "I guess that's cool."

"Also," Alice said. "I forgot to tell you but last week we got this assignment where we got to retell a famous children's book in our words. And I talked about *The*

Giving Tree!" *The Giving Tree* had been one of her and Cassidy's favorite books when they were little, although Alice had a hard time reading it now because it made her sad. So in her version, she wrote it so that the tree was actually a human mom who gave everything she had to her kids but without all that depressing letting-herself-be-cut-down stuff.

"Huh!" Cassidy said, not turning her head away from the window.

"Is everything okay?" Alice asked. "I guess this stuff is pretty boring."

"No, sorry," Cassidy said, looking back at Alice and smiling with her lips together. "I'm glad you're having a good time in school. I'm just upset about this French thing. It spoiled my whole day."

"I know what you mean," Alice said, remembering a few weeks ago when just the thought of having to read *Island of the Blue Dolphins* had ruined her night. She had learned her lesson: it just wasn't worth not getting her work done first, especially if the knowledge that she had work to do lurked over her time with Cassidy.

The bus pulled up to the girls' street, and they started walking down towards their houses, kicking at the leaves that were scattered on the sidewalk.

"You know what we might need," Cassidy said. "Mini

dance party?" Whenever the girls were feeling low or just needed to burn some energy, they turned the lights off in one of their rooms and danced as hard and as dumb and as wild as they could, to exactly four songs: two that Alice chose, and two that Cassidy chose. It was the one time Alice didn't feel self-conscious about dancing.

"I really want to," Alice said. "Really. But I can't. I've just got too much homework. Mr. Nichols gave us a new book."

"Mr. Nichols is really cramping our style," Cassidy said, frowning. "I mean, doesn't he understand that we need our BFF time?"

Alice sighed. "I know. I promise this won't last forever. It's been a busy week."

"True," Cassidy said, and picked up a perfect red leaf from the sidewalk. "It's just that this is the third day in a row that you haven't been able to hang out after school. And you used to be able to come over all the time."

"I hate it," Alice said, feeling like she wanted to cry. They were standing next to the planters on the street, which were temporarily empty. Mrs. Turner was still debating what she'd fill them with for the colder months of fall. "But I just don't know what I can do about it. The last time I didn't get to finish my work on time, I got in trouble in class, you know? Besides, isn't that what the notebook is for? So we can stay in touch?"

"Well, I hope you still have time to write in it," Cassidy teased her. "I hope you don't get too busy for it!"

"Can we just pretend like the notebook is the same as our walkie-talkies?" Alice asked. When they were little and Alice would cry when it was time for her to go home to her parents' house after spending time at Cassidy's, her dad gave her a gray plastic toy walkie-talkie set so the two could talk to each other from each other's houses, even at bedtime. They barely worked; the toys were too flimsy to get much reception and the houses were too far apart. But sometimes Alice would be able to hear Cassidy's voice through the static, and even if she couldn't understand her, it brought her comfort at night knowing her best friend wasn't far away.

Cassidy gave her hand a reassuring squeeze and the girls separated, heading towards their own houses. As Alice walked up the driveway, she started feeling mad instead of sad. It wasn't *fair*. Why did she have to be separated from the one person who totally knew how to make her feel better whenever she was down?

"Hey, what's going on?" Alice's mom asked after her

daughter entered the kitchen and angrily threw her backpack and jean jacket on the window seat. To make matters worse, the scent of fish permeated the kitchen. Mrs. Kinney was baking salmon, which Alice hated.

"I hate being in honors classes!" Alice said.

"But you were so excited about the assignments and discussions you were having in Mr. Nichols's class," Mrs. Kinney said, wiping her hands on her jeans.

"I'm sick of talking about Mr. Nichols!" Alice nearly yelled.

"Whoa," said Mrs. Kinney. "Sit down. Let's talk." She poured each of them a glass of sparkling water and fixed a lime wedge on the side, neither of which Alice really wanted, but the gesture seemed nice and the clear blue glass looked pretty with all the bubbles fizzing to the top, so she took it without complaining. They sat at the worn wooden table in the breakfast area, where hanging lighting fixtures gave the kitchen a warm feel.

"Cassidy was having a bad day and wanted to hang out after school, but I told her I had to go home to do work today. It just made me sad," Alice confessed, telling her mom all the details.

"I understand you want to see your friend, but I think that Cassidy should understand your time commitments," her mom said gently. "It's not like you get mad at her when she goes to ballet class, right? You guys find time to talk and see each other."

"Right," Alice said. "I just don't want her to think I'm blowing her off."

"You're not blowing her off," her mom said. "You just have to prioritize some things sometimes. You still see her at school, and on the bus, right? And you'll have your time back together soon. But until then, you can't be expected to do a poor job on your work just so you can see each other more than you already do."

Alice felt sad. She had homework to do, she couldn't be there for her best friend on a hard day, it didn't seem like there was anything she could do about it, *and* they were having fish for dinner.

"Do you . . . do you think it's possible that there's a little tension there because you made it into honors classes and Cassidy didn't?" Mrs. Kinney asked after taking a sip of water. She was clearly trying to choose her words delicately.

"Cass isn't stupid," Alice said angrily.

"That's not what I said at all," said Mrs. Kinney.

"You clearly want me to stop being friends with Cassidy and just be friends with dorky honors-class kids!" Alice stood up and pushed her chair away. Deep down she knew that her mom didn't mean that at all, but she felt like being mad about *something*.

"Alice," her mom said in a warning tone, but before they could talk more, Alice grabbed her backpack and stormed up to her room, slamming the door. She stood in her darkening room for a moment, not sure what to do now. Homework? Ugh.

Alicc booted up her computer, telling herself that she was going to get to work on the study questions Mr. Nichols had given them for their new book, *Animal Farm*. But first she logged onto IM, just for a second, anyway. Cassidy was online, and Alice couldn't resist the urge to talk to her best friend when she was feeling down.

AISFORALICE: Hey there. I just got into a fight with my mom ☹ Bummed about that and not being able to see each other. AND we're having fish for dinner tonight :P

BALLETCASS: That stinks! In more ways than 1.

AISFORALICE: Yeah . . . I wish we were hanging out right now. I hope things get easier soon with homework so we can see each other more!

BALLETCASS: Totally.

AISFORALICE: Sorry you had a bad day. Hugs.

BALLETCASS: Hugs back at you. Sounds like you ended up having a hard day too.

AISFORALICE: Yeah, maybe it just needs to be tomorrow.

BALLETCASS: Okay, I can't believe I'm saying this but you should get to ur hw.

AISFORALICE: I guess. You're a good friend.

BALLETCASS: I know ;) See you tomorrow.

Alice signed out, sighed, then pulled her pillow onto the floor so she could get started on the reading for class. The smell of fish wafted up from the kitchen, and she wished she had one of Mrs. Turner's forbidden incense sticks to keep the smell out of her room. Putting off her reading for just a few more minutes, she pulled the notebook out of her bag and flipped through it. To her dismay, she realized that neither she nor Cassidy had written in it for a couple of days. This would be an excellent time to write, but what did Alice have to report? *Breaking news: Homework is the worst. Salmon is the second worst.*

But that wouldn't make for a good entry. The notebook would just have to go blank another day until Alice could think of something interesting or new to say.

She sighed and flopped on her back on her bed. Up until this point, she had been able to balance her friendship with Cassidy and her schoolwork. What if it turned out that she had to pick one?

CHAPTER 9

ENTERING THE FORCE FIELD

A week later, Alice woke up feeling out of sorts, and it wasn't just the low gray sky that was getting her down. Alice had convinced herself that she'd figure out a way to see Cassidy more despite homework getting tougher, but things didn't seem to be quite working out. The day before, they had ridden the bus together and were poring over a silly celebrity gossip magazine that Tess had "borrowed" (without asking) from her older sister. The girls' favorite was the "What Were They Thinking?" section, which featured celebrities wearing highly questionable outlets.

"Oh my goodness!" laughed Tess, tapping a pink sparkly finger at a photo of an actress prancing down the sidewalk in an outfit that could only be described as pink-sequined shorteralls: overalls, but with shorts. "Cass, isn't that the *exact* same thing you tried on at the mall yesterday?"

"Well, first of all, when I tried it on, it was clearly a joke," sad Cass. "And second, you know I looked amazing in it!"

"You kind of did," said Tess. "I don't know what your secret is."

"I'm a witch!" said Cassidy, waving her fingers in the air in a somewhat witchlike motion.

"What are you guys talking about?" Alice asked, trying not to sound the way she felt, which was, specifically, five miles behind this whole conversation.

"Oh, Cass and a couple other kids from our homeroom and I went to the mall yesterday after school," said Tess.

"We were just goofing around, no big deal," added Cassidy.

"Sounds fun," Alice said, trying to smile like it didn't bother her. She and Cass used to love to go the mall and find a million stupid things to laugh about. Sometimes they had a contest where they could see how much stuff they could buy for ten dollars. If you went to the right store, you could get like seven pieces of jewelry! Admittedly, they were the kind that turned your ears green, but that wasn't the point.

"Oh, girl," Cassidy said, laying her head on Alice's shoulder. "I'm sorry. I hope you don't feel left out. It was just a spur-of-the-moment thing, and I assumed you had too much homework to do."

"It's true." Alice sighed. "I did." But still, it would have been nice to be asked. She and Cassidy hadn't been to the mall together since the summer, before school started, and she wondered when they'd go again. An uncomfortable little sensation had started gnawing in her stomach that there was something not quite right with their friendship. They weren't in a fight, but they weren't in sync the way they usually were.

To make matters worse, Alice hadn't had a spare second to write in the notebook in the last couple of days. She'd leave it as a "treat" for the end of the night, but then she was always too tired to think of anything clever to write. She worried that the friendship was like the notebook: if she took too much time away from it, it would be forgotten.

In the meantime, classes were starting to kick Alice's butt, which was a new feeling to her. First, they were studying the makeup of cells in biology, and there were way more things to remember than Alice was used to. What the heck was the difference between mitochondria and a Golgi apparatus? She worried she'd never get it straight. Meanwhile, Mr. Nichols had assigned *Animal Farm* to the class, a book about talking animals that was way freakier than a book about talking animals *should* be. Even worse, the students' assignment was to look up the Russian Revolution and write a paper comparing the different animals to what happened in Russia.

"But we haven't even *studied* the Russian Revolution yet!" Aaron Woolsey cried out, not even bothering to raise his hand. "How are we supposed to know anything about it?"

Mr. Nichols smiled and went to the board, writing the letters *L-I-U* on the chalkboard.

"Liu? Who was that, like, one of the fighters in the revolution?" Christy Gillespie asked.

Mr. Nichols smiled again, seeming to relish what he was about to impart upon them. "*L-I-U* stands for 'look it up' and is something you should get used to doing in my class." The Nerd Herd groaned. "And a word of caution before you head right to Wikipedia. You can't trust everything you read on the internet. You never know when a teacher with too much time on his hands might go online and start filling in some fun fake historical facts. So go to the library. Your parents might be able to explain to you what an encyclopedia is, if you've never heard of one."

• • •

"Whoa," Mr. Kinney had said, eyebrows up, when Alice complained about the assignment to him over meat loaf and mashed potatoes. "That's hardcore."

"Don't say 'hardcore,'" Alice said. "It makes you sound weird."

"Pardon me," Mr. Kinney said. "What I meant to say is 'That sounds like a tough assignment.' Is it okay if I say that?"

Alice rolled her eyes, even though she wasn't really mad at her dad. She just felt out of her element. She wasn't used to feeling challenged like this, like she might actually *not do well* on this assignment. That was practically unheard-of.

To try and get a grip, Alice took the early bus to school to get a little bit more reading and research done before class began. She wouldn't want to do it all the time, but it was kind of nice to be on the quiet bus, with only a few students heading in early for sports practice or extra help. Despite the gloomy weather, a morning of reading might actually be okay.

However, when she got to homeroom early, she was surprised to discover that she didn't have the room to herself, like she expected. Nikki Wilcox sat at her desk with her head on her arms. Her long black curls covered her face, but based on the way her shoulders were shaking, it looked like she was . . . crying?

Part of Alice instinctively wanted to ask Nikki if everything was okay. *Force field!* she remembered. What if Nikki bit her head off? It was probably best just to leave her alone. But before Alice could silently back out of the room, Nikki lifted her head to blow her nose.

"Oh," Nikki said, looking at Alice blankly. "Sorry." Her eyes were puffy and her normally porcelain-fair skin was flushed and blotchy.

"Sorry for what?" Alice asked, taking a hesitant step towards Nikki, who was now gathering her long hair in a ponytail in her hand and fanning the back of her neck with it.

"Um, I don't know," Nikki said. "For being weird? Just ignore me." Her flat voice, paired with the stuffiness in her nose, made her sound miserable.

"Is . . . everything okay?" Alice asked, despite Nikki asking her to ignore her.

Nikki sighed. "It's fine. It's just . . . I'm having a hard time with math right now."

"*You?*" Alice asked incredulously. She couldn't believe Miss Perfect could have a hard time with anything, let alone admit to such a thing. Nikki's face crumpled.

"Not everyone is as naturally good at math as you

are, Alice," she sniffled. "I'm sorry if that's hard for you to believe."

"No, no, that's not what I meant," Alice said. This is what she got for trying to be nice. But instead of scowling and looking away, Nikki kept her dark brown eyes on her. "It's just that . . ." Alice tried to think of a diplomatic way of saying, "You act like you know better than us all the time—that was a mask?"

"You seem so confident all the time."

"Ha," Nikki said bitterly. "Yeah, well, I definitely am not."

Alice sat down at a nearby desk, unsure how to proceed. She sighed, thinking of her mom, who always tried to see the best in everyone, and decided to shut off the force field momentarily

"What part of the math homework is giving you a hard time?"

Nikki sighed. "I just have no idea how to keep track of all these stupid shapes! Triangles, parallelograms, trapezoids, cubes—volume, circumference, surface area. They all just swim past my eyes and I freak out and feel so overwhelmed. I am *definitely* going to bomb the next test, and I'm never going to hear the end of it from my parents."

Alice couldn't believe it. She had never for a second

thought that Nikki would have ever had any problems with the schoolwork. Nikki never asked questions in class, and since she stayed to herself, Alice had never heard her talk about being worried with the other students. For that matter, Alice couldn't even imagine Nikki having parents. Alice had always just sort of envisioned her staying on the bus all night, not even sleeping but just curling up in her seat at the end of the day and powering down.

"I'm having a hard time too," Alice admitted. "This *Animal Farm* assignment is freaking me out."

"What are you talking about?" Nikki asked, in fake shock. "L-I-U, Alice. Just L-I-U!"

Alice laughed. Who knew Nikki Wilcox had a sense of humor?

"So what's your secret for knowing all that math stuff?" Nikki asked.

"I just have weirdly good memorization skills, I guess," Alice said. "A couple little tricks. It's kind of like a game."

"A lame game," Nikki said.

Oh, Alice thought. *There's Negative Nikki again.* But then Nikki surprised her. "Maybe . . . maybe sometime you could show me some of those tricks?"

"Sure," Alice said, surprised. *Wait, did I just agree to*

potentially, voluntarily, hang out with Nikki Wilcox?

The homeroom began to fill up with the rest of the class and Ms. Garrity began the announcements. Alice kicked herself for wasting the effort of waking up and coming in early, only to get no work done on the *Animal Farm* assignment. But she felt better, though, talking to Nikki, knowing that she wasn't the only one having a tough time with honors work. Idly, Alice's gaze wandered over to her. Nikki scowled at something she was writing in her notebook. She flipped her pencil around, erased furiously, and glared again, blowing an errant curl away from her face. She glanced up, saw Alice, and gave a tiny smile.

Are there two sides to Nikki Wilcox? Alice pondered. *Maybe even more?* The tough, superior-seeming girl was possibly disguising a softer side. Alice wondered what else she didn't know about her.

Just wait till I tell Cassidy! Alice thought, pulling out the notebook, grateful to finally have some news to report. But as she flipped open to a blank page, she stopped, her pen hovering over the page. Nikki was struggling just like she was, and she had confided in Alice when she didn't have to. Maybe it wouldn't be the nicest thing in the world to blab to Cassidy about it. Alice wouldn't like Nikki telling *her* friends (if she had any) about the fact that she was having a hard time with the reading. Plus, anyway, there were only a few minutes left in homeroom, Alice reasoned. She didn't have time to write the whole story out. Maybe later.

The bell toned for class change. Maybe Mr. Nichols would give them some sort of hint today that might make the assignment easier. Alice's thoughts drifted back to Nikki. She wondered if it would be easier to keep Nikki's struggles a secret for now, because Cassidy might say something like "Wait, I don't understand. First Nikki's the biggest pain in your life—now you feel sorry for her and are offering her help?" It might just be too confusing.

As the classes switched rooms, Cassidy ran up to Alice. "Hey! It was weird not riding the bus with you. Did you get your reading done eventually?"

"Uh . . . yeah!" Alice said, deciding it would be awkward to say that she didn't without explaining why.

"Cool. Well, you're not the only overachiever on the street. I'm going to get some help with French during lunch, so I won't get to see you. I'll write you, okay?"

"I haven't had the chance to write yet," Alice confessed, handing Cassidy the notebook.

"No worries. You've been busy!" Cassidy disappeared into her next class. But once the day was over,

Alice didn't get the chance to get the notebook back and see what—if anything—Cassidy had written her. After ten minutes of craning her head, looking for Cassidy's smiling face to appear between the bus aisles, the doors shut, ferrying Alice back to her street—alone.

Why didn't she tell me she wasn't taking the bus home today? Alice wondered. *Maybe she was mad at me for not riding with her this morning. Maybe she had a doctor's appointment. Maybe she somehow knew I was talking to Nikki.*

But that last part was silly. Right?

BIG NEWS

"What do you girls want on your pizza?" asked Mrs. Turner, holding a finger to her palm like she was writing down an order. She didn't actually have to write anything down, because she knew what each girl was going to order, but she still liked to ask them, for old times' sake. Alice and Cassidy were doing a minihang: they would have dinner, but no sleepover, since Cassidy had to go visit her grandparents in the suburbs the next day, Something was better than nothing, though. Plus: pizza!

"*She* is going to have half pineapple, because she's crazy," Cassidy said, pointing a newly wet purple fingernail at Alice, who was bent over, trying the same color on her toenails.

"And *she* is going to have half spinach, because she's gross," Alice said, pointing the nail-polish brush back at Cassidy.

"Okay, just making sure," Mrs. Turner said. "Pizza in about an hour."

"O-kay!" the girls singsonged, and giggled.

"Please don't drip anywhere—my mom's going to kill me if I stain the carpet," Cassidy said, looking worriedly over at Alice. "Here." She slid something over to Alice.

"You want me to use the *notebook* as a nail-polish shield?" Alice asked, dismayed but still daintily resting her toes on the brown cardboard back cover of it.

"I'm not throwing it in the trash or anything," said Cassidy. "Besides, it might as well be good for something!"

Alice frowned. "It bums me out that it's being abandoned, so sad and lonely."

"Oh, don't look like that," said Cassidy. "I'm just teasing you. We'll get back to it. Besides, we're hanging out right now, and maybe the nail polish will, you know, give it a fresh new look." She scooted next to Alice and painted a flower on the back cover with some pink polish.

"That does look pretty good," admitted Alice.

"I'm an artistic genius, what can I say?" Cassidy asked. Alice smiled. She had to admit that if it was between the notebook and actually spending time with her best friend, nothing beat the real thing. Before coming over, Alice had made a mental list of all the news for them to catch up on (especially things that were *not* Nikki related): how ballet class was going, the Nerd Herd, thoughts on what to put together for their upcoming annual Halloween scary-movie-a-thon, plus making lots of plans for Alice to look forward to—they hadn't gone to the mall, or out to Walker Bros. restaurant for pancakes, or done a clothing swap, or taken a stroll downtown while window-shopping—in *ages*.

"Speaking of artistic genius," Cassidy said. "I have big news."

"Oh yeah?" Alice looked up.

"I'm doing the school musical!" Cassidy gushed, getting so excited that she jumped up and did a leap nearly all the way across her bedroom. "I tried out last week, and then yesterday after school they posted the results, and I got in! Mr. Shankman said I had a really strong audition. I mean, everyone who auditions gets to be a part of it in *some* way, but not everyone gets to *perform*. Tess got stuck with just doing makeup. I'm actually *in* the show—*and* he gave me a solo! Not a big one, but still! I'm the only one in our grade who got one!"

"You're what?" Alice asked, confused. Normally she and Cassidy talked at length before trying anything new: an outfit, a class, a hairstyle. Not, like, that Cassidy needed to get Alice's permission, but Alice just felt out of the loop. Maybe she had been asleep or something when Cassidy had talked about it before?

"We're all doing it!" Cassidy sang with a twirl.

"We *are*?"

"Well, I mean, you know, me and Xia and Evie and April," Cassidy said hastily. The minute she said it, Cassidy looked like she might have made a mistake. "Everyone from . . . my class."

"Oh," said Alice. This was the first time she'd ever heard Cassidy say "we" and not have it involve her. She put on her proudest, most supportive face. "Well, that's awesome! I can't wait to see you perform. I bet next year you'll have the lead!" Alice didn't feel as excited as she tried to sound, though. She felt a little left out.

Alice must have been doing a great acting job, though, because Cassidy gushed on. "It's going to be so fun. I mean, it'll be cheesy—it's an eighties musical revue, but so what. Our costumes will be really silly, like metallic wigs and glow-in-the-dark jewelry and crazy makeup and stuff, but you know me, I love being goofy like that."

"I'm . . . I just don't remember you talking about it," Alice stammered.

"I *have* been, like, for weeks, silly," Cassidy said. "Maybe you were just caught up with homework or the Nerd Herd or something."

Alice smiled. Even though her feelings were a little bit hurt, she kept her mouth shut.

"The best part is, Jesse's doing stage crew for it," Cassidy said, sitting back down on the floor and hugging one of the throw pillows. "So I'll get to see him more too."

"That sounds awesome!" Alice felt like cold cement was filling up her stomach. What she really wanted to say was, "Why didn't you ask me to try out?"

"I would have asked you to audition too," Cassidy said hurriedly, like she could read Alice's mind. "But I just assumed you were too busy. Maybe you can bring the Nerd Herders to come check out the show!"

"Yeah," said Alice. But the Nerd Herd was a school group. They didn't see each other all the time and talk about everything, and she hadn't known them since she was superlittle, like with Cassidy. Maybe what Alice needed was her own thing, like the musical or some other club, but she still hadn't figured out what "her" thing was.

"I hope you're not upset," Cassidy said. "I just know that stage stuff isn't your thing, right?"

This was true, and Alice couldn't deny it. It was one thing to sing along in their bedrooms to the radio, but that was just the two of them. Ever since the piano recital incident, no way. Alice even got a little nervous in class when she was asked to read out loud. But still, she wouldn't have minded being *asked*—maybe Alice could have done stagecraft or helped hand out programs or something like that. Even if she had said no, just being asked would have been nice.

"When does it open?" Alice asked. Maybe if she got more interested in the show, she'd be able to shake this blue feeling. She was supposed to feel excited for and supportive of her best friend, not whatever *this* was.

"November," Cassidy said. "Promise me you'll come and cheer me on opening night? I won't be able to sing a single note if I don't know that my best friend is out there to support me."

"I'll cheer loudest of all," Alice said, and finally she meant it.

"Just one thing really stinks, though," Cassidy said. She flicked something invisible off her gauzy purple skirt. "I can't hang with you after school or even on the bus until the show starts, because of rehearsal."

"*What?*" Alice asked. Between Cassidy's dance classes and all of Alice's homework, it had been hard to spend much time together, but at least they always had the fifteen or so minutes between school and home to catch up.

"I know," Cassidy said. "But it'll fly by before we know it. There's always lunchtime. And besides," she said, picking the notebook up from beneath Alice's toes and fanning her feet with it. "We'll be able to catch up this way, right?"

"Yeah . . . ," Alice said, but they'd already been having a hard time keeping up. "How are you going to have time to write in the notebook, with all this rehearsing?"

"We'll figure something out," Cassidy said. "We always do. Besides, you're plenty busy yourself, right? It's a good thing! We might not be able to write as frequently, but we'll have more stuff to catch up on."

"You're right," Alice said, but she just couldn't help feeling a little bit gloomy. She knew it was ridiculous, and tried to get herself psyched for Cassidy's accomplishments, but the fact that she couldn't feel as enthusiastic as she knew she should just made her feel sadder. What kind of friend was she?

"Don't sweat it," Cassidy said, nudging Alice

playfully. "In fact . . . ," she said, and got up and cued something on her computer. "Don't stop believin'!" She started hopping around the room, singing loudly to the eighties song that apparently was part of the musical, pointing at Alice as if the song was about her. Bagel nosed open the partially closed door and began zooming around the room, yipping at an ear-bleeding volume while Cassidy performed. Alice suppressed the urge to let a Nikki-style pout creep over her face. *I kind of hate this song,* she thought.

"How was Cass?" asked Mr. Kinney, who was washing dishes when Alice got home.

"Fine," Alice said. She didn't feel like talking about all the new and exciting ways she and Cassidy were growing apart.

"You got a phone call," her mom said, too focused on her crossword puzzle to look up.

"A phone call?" Alice said, wondering aloud who could have called. She was just *at* Cassidy's.

"Yeah," Mrs. Kinney said, right as Alice read the name scrawled on the yellow pad next to the phone.

"Nikki Wilcox?" Alice said, full of disbelief.

"I know, can you believe it?" her dad asked as he tried to magically fit two more plates into an already-full dishwasher. "Nikki Wilcox. Nikki Wilcox! *THE* Nikki Wilcox. Just one thing. Who's Nikki Wilcox?"

"Don't mind him," Alice's mom said, still not looking up. "He had some coffee-flavored ice cream, and now he's out of control."

Alice rolled her eyes. Her parents were strange. Her friendship with Cassidy was strange. Nikki Wilcox—and the fact that she had called Alice— was strange. And the strangest thing was, Alice was going to call Nikki back, and was kind of excited to do so. She needed someone to talk to. Even if it was Nikki Wilcox.

CHAPTER 11

ENEMY TERRITORY?

It was Monday afternoon, and in a freak twist of North Shore weather, the sun peeked merrily through the clouds while a warm October rain drizzled down. Of course strange weather *would* be over Alice's head, because who should she be walking down the street with but Nikki Wilcox?

Just the week before, Alice had felt like she was saying good-bye to Cassidy, for the time being, anyway, as she disappeared into the world of rehearsals. Simultaneously, Alice found herself talking to the one person in school she would have never expected to. But whatever weird feelings Alice had about this moment, she had to keep them to herself. Between her and Cassidy's busyness and the fact that Alice wasn't sure how Cassidy would react to Alice hanging out with Negative Nikki, she couldn't quite bring herself to tell her best friend about her new possible friend.

On Friday, after Alice had come home from Cassidy's, she and Nikki made awkward small talk over the phone about how hard school was getting, between math and *Animal Farm*. "Um, so, want to come over after school on Monday and see if we can put our heads together?" Nikki had asked.

Alice had said sure without even thinking about it. It wasn't like she had much else going on, social-wise, plus there was a part of her that was irresistibly curious about Nikki. Would she suddenly revert back to her negative self and snap at Alice and kick her out? Or had Alice pegged her all wrong? Maybe she'd learn why Nikki didn't want to be part of the Nerd Herd. Maybe she'd learn *anything* about Nikki, because so far Alice didn't know much, aside from what she'd learned from their latest interactions: that Nikki had a hard time at math and took her schoolwork pretty seriously.

So, after school, while Cass was at musical rehearsal, Alice and Nikki got off the bus together and walked to Nikki's parents' building. Even though it was only a few blocks away from her house, it felt like several miles, after all the years just dashing across the street to Cassidy's house—sometimes without even wearing shoes!

The girls walked in silence for about a half a block,

not totally sure what to talk about, until they walked past a well-dressed older woman walking a tall, skinny dog. Suddenly Nikki brightened. "This is Edgar, isn't it?" she asked the owner, who smiled politely. "Is it okay if I give him a treat?"

"Of course," said the lady. Nikki knelt down on the sidewalk in front of this rickety, striped old dog, petted him gently on the head, and whispered to him, "Hi, Edgar. Hi, good boy. Do you want a treat?" To Alice's surprise, Nikki pulled a dog biscuit from her pocket and fed it to him.

"You, uh, carry dog biscuits around in your pockets?" Alice asked.

Nikki blushed. "Yeah. Kind of nuts, huh? But I just love dogs, especially the ones in my neighborhood, like old Edgar here. He used to be a racing dog, and he's in retirement, isn't he?"

"Yes, and thanks to you, he's loving every minute of it," says his owner.

"Okay, bye, Edgar!" Nikki said as they walked on. "Aren't dogs just the best?"

"I wouldn't know," Alice said. "I'm allergic, myself. I can't really touch them much, or else I start sneezing all over the place."

"Oh, that stinks," Nikki said. "I'm kind of obsessed.

I probably know more about dogs than any normal person should. Did you know that greyhounds are one of the oldest breeds in the world and were even mentioned in the Bible?"

"No, I certainly did not," said Alice, who couldn't decide whether this information was interesting or weird.

"I guess that's not really common knowledge or anything," said Nikki. "Here's us." Nikki and her parents lived in a redbrick apartment building with large glassed-in sunrooms. Alice had been driven by dozens of times before without really noticing. After unlocking three heavy doors, the girls hiked the three floors. Alice tried to act like she wasn't completely out of breath. Maybe this was what kept Nikki in such good shape for ballet.

"Wow," Alice said, once she stepped inside the Wilcoxes' house. "Your place is really cool." And it was—unlike the Kinneys' cheery and comfy house or the Turners' sumptuous, scented home, the Wilcox house looked like it came from one of the modern design catalogs Alice's parents got. It had clean white walls and a tidy rectangular gray couch and a funky black rug that looked like the hair of a Muppet. The dining room table was on big industrial wheels and the chairs were clear and see-through.

"Thanks," said Nikki. "Actually I picked out some of that stuff. If I get straight A's, my parents let me help decorate."

"It helps that she has good taste," said a woman who stepped out from a home office. "Hi, I'm Donna Wilcox."

"Hi, I'm Alice," Alice said, surprised by how strong Mrs. Wilcox's grip was, as well as by her hair, which was almost the opposite of Nikki's, a sleek silver bob instead of anything curly or tangly.

"Honey, come meet Nikki's new friend," Mrs. Wilcox called back to the office.

"Hang on, one second." Alice heard grumbling. Finally a tall, angular man with a shock of dark, springy hair appeared, pushing glasses up his nose. *Ah, that's where she got the hair.*

"Dr. Wilcox," he said, also shaking Alice's hand. "Technically my wife is also Dr. Wilcox, so I hope you don't get us mixed up." He chuckled to himself, and Alice smiled weakly and tried to pretend he was making her laugh.

"Dad, stop being weird," Nikki said.

"Pretty sure that's impossible!" Nikki's mom said with a laugh.

"What are you girls doing this afternoon?" Nikki's dad asked.

"Just working on math and English," Nikki said.

"Nikki tells us you're quite the math genius," he said, fixing his eyes intensely on Alice.

"Uh, well. Not really," Alice said. "I mean, I'm okay at it." What was she going to do, say, "Yes, I'm a math genius, and pretty awesome in general as you can tell"?

"Well, we appreciate whatever help you can give Nikki," he said. "We can't wait to see her make us proud at the math tournament in November."

"Right," Alice said, somehow unsurprised that Nikki's parents would actually be excited for a math tournament.

"All right," Nikki said. "Maybe you guys should let us get to work,"

"We're here if you need us!" said Nikki's mom while she and her husband retreated to their office.

"They're obsessed with their work," Nikki said, rolling her eyes. "I'm pretty sure that if they didn't share an office, they would hardly see each other."

"What do they do?" Alice asked.

"Dad's an engineer and mom works in the chemistry department, both at the University of Chicago," Nikki said. "And believe it or not, they met in math class in high school. So they're basically the original Nerd Herd. I think that's why they expect that I always get, like, straight A's all the time. *They* were the ones who got me to join the math team, because they figured it would help sharpen me up, and I don't know, maybe they think that's where I will meet my future husband. Who knows? I wish they didn't care about it so much."

Before Alice could process any of this, Nikki asked, "Are you hungry?"

"Sure," Alice said. "Always."

Nikki opened the refrigerator door, but Alice could only see a cruel joke when it came to snacks: a plate with some limp celery sticks and some ancient-looking orange slices.

"That looks . . . ," Alice tried to think of a word that was not rude that would also not be a lie. "Disgusting" was rude, but "good" was a lie.

"I know," Nikki said, closing the door. "Pretty lame, snack-wise, huh? They both have such a long commute and work so much they don't have much time to shop, so it's kind of an adventure when it comes to scrounging."

"That stinks," Alice said, suddenly grateful for her mom, who at least tried fun new things like serving breakfast for dinner or coaxing Mr. Kinney to grill hamburgers out back, even in the wintertime.

"Yeah," said Nikki. "What do your parents do?"

"My mom is an accountant who works from home, and my dad works in advertising downtown," Alice said.

"So you're lucky, they are pretty close by," Nikki said, sighing. "It's pretty unusual that my parents are home so early today. A lot of times I don't see them until dinner or later."

"Wow," said Alice, starting to realize there was even more to Nikki than she had initially assumed.

"Anyway," Nikki said, brushing her hand in the air like she was getting rid of a cobweb. "Let's do some math!" She swung her arm like she was about to start square dancing, and Alice couldn't help but laugh.

The afternoon passed much more quickly than Alice had expected. First, she had a hard time actually sitting down to focus on the homework, because she was fascinated by Nikki's room. Like the rest of the condo, it was actually *decorated*, and in a sophisticated way Alice could never have dreamed of. Tucked away too, in little corners of the room, were tiny collections of pretty objects like polished stones, heart-shaped pieces of sea glass, and kitschy plastic snow globes. Alice spent nearly an hour asking Nikki about where she got all her various items—her parents had each had fellowships at other universities, so she'd spent a good amount of time traveling.

"They're both tenured now," she said. "So we're here to stay."

The walls were painted a dark charcoal gray, the comforter an egg-yolk yellow, and the furniture an artistic-looking white, which included a white cardboard deer's head mounted on the wall.

"He's my *deer* friend," Nikki explained. "Get it? Wait, you probably do. You're in honors classes." Alice laughed again.

"You're a lot different here than in school," Alice said without thinking.

"What do you mean?" asked Nikki, stretching her legs out on the white sheepskin rug. She looked curious, not mad.

"Sometimes you just seem . . ." Alice searched for a word that was nicer than "mean" or "superior." She went with "intimidating."

"Intimidating!" Nikki said with a short laugh. "I *wish* I was intimidating."

"Well," said Alice. "It's just that, like, you don't seem like you really enjoy it when we goof around in school, even when it's part of the class, like with Mr. Nichols."

Alice decided not to mention what Cassidy had said about Nikki correcting her in ballet.

Nikki nodded. "It's not that I am annoyed by people having fun. I'm just . . . if I bring home anything other than an A in a class, my parents want to have this big long *talk* about it. They don't get mad about it, but they're both so, like . . ." She bent her arms like a robot and talked in a monotone. "'Work. Science. Math. Computer. Error.' They think there has to be an explanation for everything. I don't want to have a *talk* about why I didn't get a good grade on something. So I guess I'm just trying to avoid having that conversation— there's a part of me that freaks, like if we spend too much time joking around in class, we're going to miss something and I'm going to fall behind."

"Oh, come on," said Alice. "You're so smart. When was the last time you got a C in anything?"

"The last time we moved," Nikki said quietly, picking a piece of fuzz off the carpet with her fingernails. Alice noticed they were decorated with black polish that was chipping off at the tips. "It's hard. You know, most of you guys have known each other since you were bitty babies, but I've only lived here for a few years. I still feel like the odd girl out."

Alice nodded. This explained a lot. "But you live

here *now*, right? For good? You're not the new girl anymore."

"That's true," said Nikki thoughtfully. "I guess that's true."

Finally they got to work, with just enough time for Alice to walk Nikki through a few memorization tricks she had for various formulas and for Nikki to show Alice some resources she'd found that explained, in (sort of) easy terms, what had happened in the Russian Revolution.

"Spoiler alert," Alice said, frowning. "Now I think I know how *Animal Farm* is going to end."

"Yeah," said Nikki. "If I were an animal, I'd rather live with Old MacDonald, personally."

"For real," said Alice. "Now, if I can just remember what on earth a mitochondria does, I might do okay in biology too."

"I have a weird way of remembering that," said Nikki. "Mitochondria help with cellular respiration. You know, like breathing. So I think, *I might breathe today: mitochondria!*" Alice laughed. She felt so tempted to ask Nikki why she wasn't this funny and silly and helpful in class, but she decided to keep it to herself. For now.

Nikki's mom emerged again from her office. "Alice, don't you have to get home to your parents?" She frowned. "It's nearly six p.m. Don't you think they'll be worried about you?"

"Mom." Nikki sighed.

"It's okay," Alice said. "I should go. But no, I don't think they'd be worried—I mean, I don't live that far away, and I said I'd be home for dinner by six fifteen."

Dr. Wilcox smiled but looked pointedly at Nikki, who sighed again. "Come on, Alice," she said. "I'll walk you downstairs."

"Bye, Alice!" Nikki's mom said. "I hope you come by again soon."

The girls left and began their way down the hall stairs. "Sorry about that," Nikki whispered. "My mom can be so uptight."

"It's okay," said Alice. "I mean, I should get going anyway."

"I think they just assume your parents are as crazy as they are. They're pretty overprotective since they don't know where I am all the time," Nikki explained. "If I'm not home from ballet by six, they have one of the neighbors call them at work so they can start freaking out. Which stinks, because I know everyone hangs out after class, but if I don't go right away, I'll get in big trouble."

That explains a lot, thought Alice. "What about when you just want to go over to your friends' houses?" she asked. "Are they okay with that?"

"Oh, um," Nikki said as she rubbed at a chip in the wooden banister. "I don't really have any friends— nearby anyway. So I guess that makes things easier on my parents."

"Oh," Alice said. She felt sorry for Nikki but didn't want to say so.

"I mean," Nikki said hastily as she and Alice stepped out of the lobby onto the sidewalk. "I don't want you to throw me a pity party. It's just something I'm used to."

"But why?" asked Alice. She could understand if Nikki were still new, but she was on the North Shore to stay, and by and large, everyone in their grade seemed pretty nice.

"Oh, look!" said Nikki. A man with a tiny white dog approached them on the street. "It's Muffin! Hi, Muffin!"

"Hi, Nikki!" said Muffin's owner.

Nikki crouched down to pet Muffin and give him a few of the treats from her pocket. "Doesn't it seem like if you had a dog, you'd always have someone who would be there for you when you're sad?" Nikki said to Alice. "But I can't get one because my parents don't think I'm up to taking care of one—and they definitely don't want to."

After Muffin and his owner moved on, she looked at her feet. "And the reason I don't have a lot of friends? Well. I don't know. I think it's the moving thing. Because of my parents' jobs, I've lived in four different cities so far. And it really stunk to make friends with someone and then move on. I guess I figured with the last couple of moves that it's easier not to make friends than to make friends and leave right away."

"But you're here now, right?" asked Alice. "You said so yourself. You're not going anywhere for a while. So maybe it's okay to get to know people."

"Maybe," said Nikki, and smiled.

Alice got home that night feeling unusual, but not in a bad way—it had seemed, for the last few months, she'd had only two settings: Cassidy Time or School Time, and now she had found a new, unnamed state of being. She'd gone out and actually spent time with someone from school, but she didn't feel freaked out about being behind on her work either. Not to mention that it seemed within the realm of possibility that Nikki Wilcox was not only a functional member of society but also, it seemed, secretly a nice, funny girl hidden beneath some defensive walls. Would wonders never cease?

Upstairs, in her room after dinner, Alice was just getting into the homework zone when she heard a *ping* from her computer. She looked up from her bed, where she was reading (above the covers—she'd learned her lesson).

> **NKWLCX:** Hey! That was fun! Can we do it again soon?

Alice's instant messenger must have automatically turned on when she powered up the computer. She didn't even have time to get to her desk and respond until she heard several more *ping*s.

> **NKWLCX:** This is Alice, right? I got your IM from the school directory.
> **NKWLCX:** If this is not Alice, I apologize for being weird.

Alice laughed to herself and sat down in her desk chair.

AISFORALICE: Hey! It is me. You are kind of weird but not TOO weird. ☺
NKWLCX: Ha! What are you up to?
AISFORALICE: Actually, I'm doing hw. Sorry, I didn't mean to turn on my IM. I probably shouldn't be chatting right now. But yes, I would like to hang out again soon!
NKWLCX: Ah. Sorry to bother you! ☺
NKWLCX: I was just psyched to see you online. My buddy list is short. ☺

Alice cringed a little bit. She didn't quite know how to process this information. Nikki actually seemed pretty well adjusted for someone who freely admitted that she didn't have a lot of friends, but at the same time, Alice didn't know that she'd talk about it so much if it were her.

Alice sat back in her chair and pondered how lucky she was to have parents who were so relaxed (at least in comparison), to have Cassidy as her best friend (even if they weren't seeing each other as much as usual), and even to have the Nerd Herd. She didn't have as much to complain about as she thought she did. She had an idea.

AISFORALICE: Tell you what. Later this week, let's do another study session, but this time on MY turf. I'm taking you to Walker Bros. so we can have some REAL brain food.
NKWLCX: What's Walker Bros.? Either way, I'm in!
AISFORALICE: It's basically the happiest place on earth.
NKWLCX: That sounds *pretty* good. See you tomorrow!

Alice signed off and let herself spend a moment fantasizing about Walker Bros., a breakfast spot that she and Cassidy had been going to since they were little. There, the air smelled like syrup and coffee, busboys in white hats bustled about, and the wooden tables were all comfortingly sticky and cozy. She smiled to herself, thinking about how each and every time they went, both she and Cassidy agonized over what to order, but they always got the same thing: chocolate chip pancakes for Alice, strawberry waffle for Cassidy.

Time to get to work. Alice dumped her backpack

onto her floor. She felt guilty as the notebook called out to her—*Hey, remember me?* Alice felt a pang that she hadn't written in it, and almost that she was keeping a secret from Cassidy, because she could write so much about Nikki, her parents, her dog obsession, her loneliness. Cassidy would die! But the notebook stayed closed.

After about an hour of homework, Alice heard a knock on her door.

"Hey, kid," her dad said. "Want to go nuts and go get some ice cream? It's nice out, and your mom and I are feeling wild and crazy."

"Sure!" Alice said, glad that she had gotten her work over with. The Kinneys walked the three blocks to the ice cream parlor, discussing along the way what type of ice cream they'd get so as to optimize maximum tasting ability. (They decided on pralines and cream for Alice's mom, rocky road for Alice's dad, and mint chip for Alice.)

"Hey, isn't that Cassidy?" Mrs. Kinney asked as they entered Sweet Treats. Alice brightened: this was going to turn out to be an extra-fun night after all. Until she saw that Cassidy was sitting at a table not with her family, but with Evie, Xia, April, and a few other girls

Alice recognized from the musical.

"Uh, hi!" Alice said, approaching their table. She wasn't sure if she was interrupting something, or not.

"Hi!" Cassidy said. She glanced quickly at the other girls, almost guiltily. They all smiled and said hi to Alice, friendly as could be. So why did she feel like the odd girl out?

"Um, so . . . ," Alice said. She couldn't think of a question that didn't sound idiotic ("Having some ice cream?") or passive-aggressive ("Having a good time without me?").

"We were just meeting up to brainstorm costume ideas for the musical," Cassidy explained hastily. "We're in charge of our own wardrobe and we wanted to make sure we looked cute—coordinated, but not too . . ."

". . . matchy-matchy?" Alice filled in, remembering their plans for their first day of school.

"Kind of," said Cassidy. "Anyway. Do you want to . . ." She gestured to the table, where there were no free seats anyway.

"No, that's fine, thanks," Alice said. "I'm here with my, um . . ." She leaned her head towards her parents, because saying "I'm here with my parents" sounded too lame.

"Okay!" Cassidy said. "Well . . . catch you tomorrow?"

"Sure," said Alice. "Catch you tomorrow." The girls smiled awkwardly and Alice got in line with her parents, even though she had kind of lost her appetite for ice cream.

"Everything okay?" Alice's dad said as they walked home. She didn't even complain when he took his usual way-too-big bite of her ice cream.

"Sure," Alice said. "Cassidy and those girls are just working on the musical."

"That's fun!" Alice's mom said brightly, and Alice could only agree. There wasn't anything wrong with Cassidy working on the musical with the kids in it—Alice wasn't in it, after all, so why should she be involved with an ice-cream meeting about wardrobe?

It's fine. Alice shrugged to herself. *Until the musical is over, Cassidy is doing her thing, and I guess I'm doing mine. There's nothing wrong with that . . . right?*

CHAPTER 12

WORLDS COLLIDE?

Alice and Nikki were making their way to the front of the quick-moving line at the Walker Bros. entrance, and Alice could already hear the clink of heavy white plates and mugs, the *ching* of the cash register up front. They'd successfully made it through the *Animal Farm* section of Mr. Nichols's class, each getting a "goodish" grade on the paper (they agreed not to reveal to each other what grades they got on their work, an idea of Nikki's that surprised Alice, who would have taken her for a more competitive person), and decided the end of the week was a good time to celebrate.

Plus, they could work some more on their math problems: Nikki had been informed she'd be a starter on the math meet coming up. She wasn't exactly excited about it, but she *was* excited about the idea of pancakes after school.

"I can't *believe* you haven't been here before," Alice said again.

"Why would I make that up?" Nikki asked, grinning. "I could come up with much more interesting lies than that."

"Prove it."

"Um. Let's see. I'm not actually a student at Lakeside Middle School. I'm a spy, sent there by the government. I am actually forty years old but just look really young. And not only *have* I been to Walker Bros. before, I own it! Welcome to my restaurant. I'm one of four brothers named Walker. I'm Walker Number Three."

Alice laughed. "But where do your parents take you for pancakes on the weekends?"

Nikki shrugged. "What can I say? You've met my parents. They don't get out much. And you've seen our kitchen; they don't exactly prioritize delicious food. If I'm lucky, I get a frozen waffle—and if it's an extraspecial day, my mom will even put it in the toaster for me."

"Well, you're in for a treat," Alice said over her shoulder, after a no-nonsense hostess signaled to the girls that she had room for two and waved them on. They settled into a tiny wooden booth that was just big enough for the both of them. One of the busboys set down some sweating glasses of water and moved on in a flash.

"Whoa," said Nikki, her eyes widening at the menu. "I'm going to need an hour to look this over. Where are the flabby celery sticks and dried-up oranges?"

"I think they only serve those on special occasions," Alice said.

"You girls ready?" asked a tired-looking waitress who looked like she didn't have a lot of time for dillydallying.

"Um," said Nikki.

"If you get the chocolate chippies, you can't go wrong," said Alice.

"Done," Nikki said.

"I'll have the apple pancake," Alice said. She decided today was a good day to try something new. Besides, she'd seen enough apple pancakes go by to know that they were basically glorified apple pies, and what could go wrong with that? "And a small orange juice."

"What if . . . ," Nikki said, scrunching her dark eyebrows together. "What if I got a hot chocolate . . . *and* chocolate chip pancakes?"

The waitress waited, her pencil in the air.

"Do it!" Alice grinned.

"It's crazy!" Nikki said. "My parents would die if they knew I was eating so much sugar!"

"I'm pretty sure hot chocolate is the only thing that goes with chocolate chip pancakes," Alice said. After being the nerd in her friendship with Cass, being the one who had to go home and do homework and who had too much stage fright to perform in public, it was fun to feel like the crazier, more outgoing one.

Nikki nodded. "Okay. That's what I'll have. But I'm holding you accountable if things get weird." She waggled her eyebrows.

"Rebels," the waitress muttered, and rolled her eyes while she scribbled a little bit. Alice didn't feel too bad about the breakfast indulgence, though. Walker Bros. was the place to pack it away. She once saw four football players from the high school order ten orders of Belgian waffles with strawberries and whipped cream—and eat them all, then ask for a follow-up side of bacon.

"So," Nikki said, and began to shred the edge of her white paper napkin. "I wanted to let you know—no pressure—that the date of our first big math meet of the season is in a few weeks. And—I know, math meet, ugh!—but if you were, like, bored or something, if you wanted to come, that would be cool. Since you've been so helpful so far with the formulas and stuff." She then blushed pink and pushed a packet of sweetener around the table with her finger like it was a toy car.

Alice was charmed by how bashful Nikki seemed to be. *Are we friends now?* she wondered. *Sure, why not.* "No problem!" Alice said. "I'll have to check with my parents, but I think I can be there."

"Okay!" Nikki said. "It's November tenth."

Something about the date sounded familiar to Alice, but she forgot about it once the drinks came. The orange juice at Walker Bros. was sweet and bright and came in the perfect-size glass, not too big but not too small. But nobody seemed as happy as Nikki did with her hot chocolate, which came topped with a mountain of whipped cream.

"Ooh," she said. "I'm almost sad to eat it. It's so beautiful." She dipped a spoon into the mug to get a bit of the drink topped with a bit of the cream.

"Ooh!" she said again when a busboy showed up with the girls' order. Nikki's pancakes were dotted with melty chocolate chips and topped with even more whipped cream, while Alice's pancake was the size and shape of a deep-dish pizza, except one that was filled with sticky caramelized apples.

"Welcome to Walker Bros.," Alice said, and they dug in.

The girls ate, in heaven, for as long as they could

before they sat back against their seats, too full to continue.

"I want to keep eating, but I'm afraid of what will happen," moaned Nikki.

"Why don't we work on some of the math stuff and take a break," suggested Alice. "Maybe we'll get a second wind after a few problems."

"The sugar will give us an energy boost!" Nikki giggled. The two pushed their plates to the side and squeezed their notebooks and textbooks onto the table. They measured angles for a little while.

"You know what would not be the worst idea in the world?" Alice said. "If two brains are better than one, maybe even more brains would be great. What if we got some other Nerd Herders together sometime? We could meet at my house and go over math and reading for Mr. Nichols's class and biology. Who knows what other cool tricks and ideas everyone else has?"

"Sure," Nikki said, but her brow was furrowed. "I mean, do you think people would be okay if I was there too?"

Alice smiled and rolled her eyes. "We're one big Herd, aren't we?" she asked. "I promise you, it'll be fun. Well, if not fun, anyway, interesting. Maybe not interesting, actually—useful? If not useful . . . at least we have an excuse to eat snacks and drink pop?"

"All right, I'm sold!" said Nikki. She then tilted her head. "Hey, do you hear that?"

Alice lifted her head. Above the general din of the other diners, the noise from the kitchen and the checkout line up front, she *did* hear something, a different, organized type of sound. It was . . . singing.

"What *is* that?" Nikki asked, looking more curious than annoyed. Some of the other diners around them seemed irritated.

"That sounds familiar," Alice said.

"Maybe it's a party or something!" Nikki said. "I'm going to go check it out."

"Okay," Alice said. She was considering taking another stab at her apple pancake when it hit her. The song was "Don't Stop Believin'," and the people singing were Cassidy and the other kids from the musical.

For the second time in a week, I'm going to look like a loser in front of all them for not being part of the show, Alice thought glumly. But then another, more urgent thought came to her: *Cassidy still doesn't know that Nikki and I have been hanging out!* She looked up in a panic to see Nikki just steps away from Cassidy's table.

Alice stood for a moment as the restaurant bustled around her, and tried to envision explaining to Cassidy just what exactly she was doing hanging out with Nikki. However, she couldn't imagine the conversation going pleasantly.

"*You're* hanging out with Negative Nikki?" she could see Cassidy asking in disbelief, while all her friends from the musical giggled.

To possibly have yet another awkward moment with Cassidy . . . in a public place, no less—not to mention hurting Nikki's feelings—would be too much for Alice.

So Alice decided to tell a little white lie.

"Nikki, wait!" she croaked, just before Nikki turned the corner into the room the singing was coming from. Nikki's colorful high-tops squeaked on the tiled floor as she came to a quick stop, her denim skirt swinging forward as if it still wanted to keep walking.

"What's up?" she asked, looking concerned.

"I don't feel so well," Alice said, willing her skin to look even paler than it already did.

"Why? What's wrong?" Nikki said, frowning. *What is wrong?* Alice thought. *Think, Alice, think!* "Is your stomach upset?"

"Yes," Alice said, almost gratefully. Her tummy *was* in knots, actually, but not for the reasons Nikki probably thought. "I think I need to go home."

"Poor thing," Nikki said, her face softening in a

way Alice hadn't seen before. "No problem. Let's head home. I was up to speed on all the math stuff for today anyway."

Fortunately, the waitress saw the girls putting on their coats and dropped off the check. "Box this up, honey?" she asked, nodding at Alice's half-eaten apple pancake.

"Probably not, if your stomach doesn't feel good," Nikki whispered.

"Oh yeah," Alice said. "I guess not," she told the waitress, and looked longingly as her sticky, caramelly, delicious apple pancake got swooped away by a busboy who was probably just going to throw it in the trash.

"All right, you all set?" Nikki asked. "Let's go." The girls started towards the front door, which Alice realized was right next to Cassidy's table. She could even catch a peek of Cassidy's red-and-black-checked fall jacket through the doorway.

"Nikki," Alice said. "I need fresh air—like, right now." And displaying a sense of drama and impulsiveness that wasn't typically her style, Alice dashed for and threw herself through the side door, prominently marked FIRE ESCAPE ONLY: ALARM WILL SOUND.

The door wasn't lying. To her horror, Alice heard a *BEEP BEEP BEEP* blaring through the restaurant after

Nikki came dashing after her. Finally the metal door closed, and it was quiet in the Walker Bros. parking lot, aside from the cars whooshing by on Green Bay Road.

"Gosh, are you okay?" Nikki asked, looking seriously concerned.

"Yes," Alice said. "I already feel better." This was true, now that she was done making a scene at her favorite restaurant, but she still felt miserable. She'd dragged Nikki out, lied to her, and was for some reason afraid of her own best friend. Alice wasn't sure she recognized herself anymore. She wasn't a liar, and she felt like she was making her friendship with both Cassidy and Nikki more complicated than they needed to be—but she didn't know how to get out of it.

"Would it help to take a walk?" asked Nikki. "Maybe get some water?"

"I think I just need to go home," Alice said.

"Okay," Nikki said. "Call me later and let me know you're doing okay?"

"Sure," Alice said, and turned and started trudging in the direction of her house. Of course—*of course*—it started drizzling. At least Alice had decided to wear her green parka with the faux-fur-trimmed hood instead of her purple puffer jacket. She pulled up her hood and sighed. She *deserved* to actually get sick for lying and being a bad friend.

Instead of walking straight home, Alice headed down to the lakefront so she could wander along the walking and biking path that led to her parents' house. In the summer, the lakefront was busy, the park packed with people playing volleyball, picnicking, sunning themselves, and walking their dogs, a place where she and Cassidy enjoyed riding their bikes or sharing some popcorn with the seagulls. Alice kind of liked having it to herself in the cooler months, though. Listening to the waves and looking at the lake, which changed color every day (today it was a deep navy blue; some other days it was gray, or silver, or aqua, or even green) typically helped her get her thoughts together.

Why, exactly, did she *panic* when she realized that she, Cassidy, and Nikki were all under the same roof together? Part of it was that Alice had felt left out when Cassidy joined the musical without telling her about it first. After running into Cassidy at the ice-cream store with her other friends, Alice didn't want to face another awkward moment.

But there was more to it than that. Alice started kicking a pinecone along the path, trying to work things out. She knew that there was still a tiny grain of weirdness between the two of them from when she had gotten into honors classes and Cassidy hadn't. And if Cassidy saw Alice with Nikki Wilcox? Maybe she'd think that Alice was just trying to get back at Cassidy for the times she hadn't been invited out for ice cream or to the mall. Plus, Cassidy didn't know Nikki the way Alice did (yet). What if Cassidy said something snarky to Nikki? Nikki was Alice's friend now, and had been so nice to her at Walker Bros. Alice didn't want to get her mixed up with Cassidy when Cassidy still didn't know the real Nikki.

Alice kicked the pinecone into the grass with the tip of her pink Dr. Marten and took a deep breath of the cool, misty air. If only there were some way to blend together Cassidy and her Nerd Herd friends . . . but unfortunately, even Alice wasn't smart enough to figure out how to make that happen.

In the meantime, though, she knew of a way to at least get Nikki more incorporated into the Nerd Herd. Once she got home, she started writing a mass email to everyone in the class.

CHAPTER 13

CASSIDY'S TURN

"Hi," Alice said, meeting Cassidy at the bus stop Monday morning.

"Hi," replied Cassidy. The two girls stood quietly, their hands gripping their backpack straps, each staring out at the street. It was possibly the first time the two had not had much to say to each other—ever. "How was your weekend?"

"Fine," Alice said. "How about yours?"

"Nice!" Cassidy said brightly. "We—I mean, us in the musical—had rehearsal and then went to Walker Bros., so that was fun."

Alice had to fight the urge to say "I know."

"I missed you, though," Cassidy added with a shy smile. "It's not the same without someone to steal my strawberry waffle."

"Hey," Alice said suddenly, coming up with a brilliant idea that was infinitely better than this current conversation, where Alice was afraid she was going to spill the beans that she had evacuated Walker Bros. in order to avoid running into her best friend. "Want to sleep over tomorrow night? Let's have old-fashioned you-and-me time. It's been too long."

"Um . . . sure!" Cassidy said. "I don't have rehearsals tomorrow night so . . . definitely!"

"Great!" said Alice, and luckily, just then, the school bus turned down the street. This could be exactly what she and Cassidy needed, although Alice felt like she had better put on a great sleepover, or else. If it felt as awkward as their last couple of encounters . . . well, they might be in trouble.

"Hey, guys," Alice announced at the end of Mr. Nichols's class. "Just a reminder. Anyone who wants to come to my house after school today for study group is welcome."

"Thanks for sending that email, Kinney," said Aaron. "I'm in."

"Me too!" Christy and Todd nodded.

"Nikki, you're in too, right?" Alice said. Nikki blushed but nodded. Alice figured that if she could get Nikki to blend in as part of the Nerd Herd, maybe she could finally get Cassidy and Nikki to coexist, too.

Ironically, for a bunch of smart kids, the Nerd Herd was kind of a flop when it came to actually functioning as a study group. All Christy, Aaron, Nikki, and Alice had been able to do since they came over to Alice's was snack on popcorn, drink pop, and goof around. "Once Todd comes, we'll get to work, promise," said Aaron.

Alice didn't mind, though, because she had other plans on her mind.

"Hey, did you know that Nikki lived in Hawaii for a little bit?" Alice announced.

"Really?" Christy asked, her green eyes widening. "You lived in paradise and now you live in . . . Illinois?"

Nikki laughed. "My parents taught there for a few years, but now they have jobs here. You know what? I like it better here. I think I like the snow. Is that crazy?"

"*Kind* of crazy," Aaron said thoughtfully. "Actually, no, I'd say mostly crazy." Everyone laughed right as the doorbell rang.

"That's probably Todd," Alice said, scrambling up. "I'll get it." She was too busy looking over her shoulder to see how Nikki was getting on with the others that she didn't even bother looking out the front door before opening it. "Todd, thank goodness you're here or else—"

But it wasn't Todd. It was Cassidy, looking a little frantic, like a squirrel that had run into traffic—it was possible she wanted to bolt but wasn't sure which way to go. She stood in the entrance, her hands dangling awkwardly by her sides, the notebook clutched in one of them.

"Uh, hi," Cassidy said. "I just wanted to bring by the notebook. I wrote a bunch in it today and figured you might want to read it tonight. I heard a bunch of voices inside. Um, what's going on?" she asked, craning her head to look into the house, where the noise of Aaron, Christy, and Nikki talking boisterously emanated from the kitchen.

"It's a Nerd Herd study group," explained Alice.

"Hi, Cassidy!" Christy called, spying Cassidy in the doorway. Cassidy waved back, uncertainly.

"So, uh . . . ," Alice said, not sure what she was supposed to do next.

"You do realize that . . . Nikki Wilcox is in your house," whispered Cassidy. "Are you doing okay?"

"Yeah," said Alice. "I had to invite her as part of the class, you know?" she said. "So she doesn't feel left out." There was a whoop of laughter from the other room, which normally would be a good sound—Nikki and the Herd were having fun!—but right now, well, Alice just looked like she was lying to Cass. Which she was.

"She sounds like she's doing okay," Cass said. "Well, I guess I should go."

"Okay," said Alice helplessly, taking the notebook from her friend. She felt mean for not including Cassidy, but what would she get out of a study group for some classes she wasn't even in?

"Cass, wait," Alice said suddenly.

"Yes?" Cassidy said, her eyebrows up hopefully.

"We're still having a sleepover tomorrow night, right?"

"Oh," Cassidy said, leaning back. "Sure. Why wouldn't we?"

She turned away, and Alice watched as Cassidy headed across the street, back to her house, her hoop earrings swaying as she walked quickly.

"Hey, Alice," Christy said, when Alice came back to the living room. "Nikki said her dad can get cheap tickets to Northwestern basketball games. Don't you think it would be fun if we all went as a group sometime?" Alice nodded. Her plan of incorporating Nikki into the Nerd Herd was going off without a hitch—but why did she feel so bad?

CHAPTER 14

A VERY IMPORTANT SLEEPOVER

The morning before Cass was due to sleep over, Alice prepped for the perfect night. If it was a good night, she would feel better about the state of Cassidy's and her friendship. If not . . . she was worried that they might be drifting in separate directions for good. Alice got together all her manicure equipment, stacked up all the magazines she had in her room to pore over, gathered some materials for homemade facials, and added a few things to her mom's shopping list.

"What's this?" her mom asked, squinting at Alice's handwriting.

"Funfetti cake mix," Alice said. "We're going to make cupcakes."

"What's Funfetti?"

"It's like edible confetti," Alice said. "Nikki told me about it. She had it when she was visiting her cousin once. She says, 'Funfetti is like a party in your mouth.'"

Mrs. Kinney laughed. "Hey, why don't you also invite Nikki over to the sleepover?"

"I can't do that!" Alice said, horrified.

"Why not?"

"Well, Nikki and Cassidy aren't exactly friends, Mom," Alice said.

"How come?" Mrs. Kinney looked at her with a raised eyebrow. "They're both nice girls. They're both smart. They're both *your* friends. Aren't they both in ballet?"

"Um, well." There was no way to sugarcoat it. "Cassidy thinks Nikki is stuck-up."

"But Nikki's *not* stuck-up."

"No."

"So," said Mrs. Kinney, "why can't you explain that to Cassidy? Or better yet, show her?"

"I just can't, Mom," Alice said, sighing dramatically. Eventually she'd figure out a way to get Nikki and Cassidy to be friends, but first she had to tell Cassidy that she and Nikki were friends. Dragging Nikki over to the slumber party was obviously not the ideal way to break the news. Just imagine, Cassidy coming over to find Nikki already there. *"Surprise! It's a Nerd Herd ambush!"*

"Doesn't Cassidy know you're friends with Nikki?".

Alice busied herself with drawing perfectly round bubbles all around the border of her mom's shopping list. "Umm . . ."

"So you have to sneak around and keep them separate?" her mom continued. "That doesn't seem like a very good plan."

"Well, Mom, you just don't get it." Alice said.

"I guess not. But this whole arrangement doesn't sound very *Funfetti* to me."

Later that morning, after Mr. Nichols's class, the bell toned for class change.

"Hey, what are you doing tonight?" Nikki asked as she threw her books into her camouflage-printed book bag.

"Oh, hanging out with Cassidy," Alice said, a little apologetically.

"Cool, can I come too?" Nikki said. Alice wished she could just say yes, but she was petrified that, unless she got the circumstances exactly right, the three girls would be like the vegetable oil, water, and corn syrup that the Nerd Herders had mixed together for Ms. Crawford's class: not blending at all.

"Um, I mean," Alice said, stammering. "We . . . we're

going to this thing . . . at the mall. We have tickets."
Alice wanted to kick herself. She had never been to a
"thing" at the mall in her life, aside from a shopping trip
or a visit to see the mall's creepy young Santa Claus.

"A concert?" Nikki asked.

Alice nodded, hoping that Nikki wouldn't ask any
more questions. She hated lying and she was pretty sure
she sucked at it. "I think it's sold out?" she squeaked.
But it was better than saying "My best friend just doesn't
like you."

"No worries," Nikki said, holding her head up
high and coolly flipping her long, dark curls over her
shoulder. "I know you and Cassidy have been friends
for forever. And I don't get the feeling she's my biggest
fan, anyway."

"What do you mean?" Alice said.

"Oh, I can just tell," Nikki said. "She rolls her eyes
sometimes when I have to bust out of ballet in a hurry
to get home for my parents' crazy curfew. And I was in
the bathroom with her the other day between classes,
and she pretended like I was invisible." Alice cringed
inside, hearing that Cassidy could be mean like that,
even if Cassidy didn't realize she was hurting Nikki's
feelings.

"She's just nervous about the musical!" Alice said.

"Maybe she just needs to get to know me better," Nikki said.

"Totally!" said Alice. That night, she resolved, she would try to get Cassidy to see the good side of Nikki.

"Well," Nikki said as they parted ways in the hall. "Maybe sometime we can all hang out. Maybe even after my math meet in a few weeks! Anyway, have fun at the mall!" She trotted off, her long hair swinging down her back. Alice smiled weakly and told herself that by the end of the weekend, she'd have everything between the two girls sorted out and there would be no more need for lies.

"Say 'fabulous'!" said Mrs. Kinney, stepping back and holding the camera up to her eye.

"Fab-u-lousss!" singsonged Alice and Cassidy in unison as Mrs. Kinney snapped a photo. And with that, another sleepover was officially under way. Ever since Alice and Cassidy's first sleepover, when Alice's mom had taken a photo of the girls in their pajamas hugging in front of the fireplace, the two had commemorated each sleepover with a photo in the same spot, filing them all in a special sleepover photo album.

The styles had changed, of course: the girls wore flannel pajama pants (pugs on Cassidy's, rainbows on Alice's) and T-shirts instead of footie pj's, and their makeup skills had grown immensely since the first time they had dabbed at each other's faces with blush from old compacts that Mrs. Kinney had loaned them.

They were such suckers for tradition that once they had forgotten to take the picture, and two days later they reconvened in the same pajamas so they could re-create the moment. And of course, now, Alice felt like it was especially important to recapture the most awesome moments of their friendship, because if they had fun, maybe they'd be able to move past the weirdness of the last few weeks.

"Awesome," said Cassidy, approving the picture on Mrs. Kinney's camera. "All that posing's made me hungry."

"Are you ready for Funfetti?" Alice asked as they headed to the kitchen.

"I'm ready for Funfetti! I'm ready for Funfetti!" Cassidy chanted. Alice laughed. For the first time in what felt like forever, she and Cassidy were back to normal. The only trick, though, was how to approach the topic of Nikki without making things awkward.

The girls danced around to the pop radio station in the kitchen as they mixed up the cupcake batter.

"Very important question. What's your *ultimate* cupcake?" Cassidy asked.

"Hmm," said Alice. "I would like to try a carrot cake cupcake someday."

"That would be good," said Cassidy. "I think my favorite still is a yellow cake cupcake with chocolate frosting."

"Mmm, chocolate," Alice said, licking a bit of icing off her finger. "Can you believe that Nikki Wilcox never had the chocolate chip pancakes at Walker Bros.—" She was going to finish saying "before I took her there last weekend?" But Cassidy interrupted her.

"Ugh, why, because she's on a *diet*?" said Cassidy, making a face.

"Um, no," said Alice, searching for a subtle way to tell Cassidy about how she and Nikki had been hanging out lately, and how she'd gotten to know her, and how she was a sweet, caring person who just needed some extra confidence and friends and understanding. But it was hard to figure out how to kick that conversation off when Cassidy was already deep into a speech about how she couldn't deal with girls who refused to eat dessert.

"It's un-American!" she said, waving around a

161

wooden spoon for emphasis. "God put sweets on this planet for a reason—because they *taste good*. I don't trust people who don't eat chocolate! It's because she's in ballet, isn't it? That's so dumb. Madame Bernard is always telling us that we need to eat to *live and love and thrive!*" Cassidy waved the wooden spoon around like she was directing an orchestra performing a song about cupcakes.

Ding! Saved by the bell. The kitchen timer went off just when Alice started to worry that Cassidy would accidentally smack her with the spoon.

"Oooh, yummy," Cassidy breathed in the vanilla scent as Alice carefully pulled out the hot muffin tin with one of her mom's old oven mitts. The girls busied themselves with mixing up the icing, and Alice thought how it was funny that Nikki's favorite cupcake was the only thing that got Cassidy to stop talking about how much she didn't like Nikki.

With the cupcakes finally iced and the sprinkles sprinkled on top of the icing, the girls took a plate and settled into the squishy dark green couch in the Kinneys' den to watch *The Princess Bride*, an old movie Mrs. Kinney had introduced them to years ago and they watched every sleepover, even though they knew every line.

"Do you think we'll ever get sick of this movie?" Alice asked.

"I'll get sick of it when I get sick of these," Cassidy said, peeling the wrapper off her second cupcake. "That is to say, in a thousand years to never." The movie, the pajamas, the cupcakes, the old striped afghan the girls cuddled under: the night was the perfect old-school sleepover—just about.

Right when the handsome Westley was about to stand up to the evil (and weird-looking) Prince Humperdinck, though, the phone rang.

"Not now!" Cassidy yelled. "This is one of my twelve favorite parts!" Alice grinned. Her mom would normally grab the phone, but she happened to glance over at the caller ID display on the end table next to Cassidy's side of the sofa. It read, in letters that seemed twelve feet high, WILCOX.

Aargh! If her mom answered, she'd announce to Alice that Nikki was on the line or, even worse, suggest that Alice invite her over. Clearly, Cassidy wasn't ready to hear that Alice and Nikki were buddies, so Alice was left with only one thing to do: perform an acrobatic feat and lunge over to the phone to silence the ringer.

"Ow!" Cassidy laughed after Alice threw herself

over Cassidy and silenced the ring. "What the heck was that all about?"

"Telemarketers, always ruining the best parts of movies!" Alice cried.

Cassidy laughed. "Maybe *you* should be in ballet, with moves like that." Alice smiled and settled back in for the rest of the movie. Truth be told, her hip hurt a little bit from throwing herself across the couch, but at least she wasn't trying to explain to Cassidy why Nikki was calling.

Once the movie ended, the girls split one last cupcake along with some milk before getting ready for bed.

Cassidy turned around and leaned against the counter after wiping off her milk mustache. "So, I know I probably don't even have to ask you this, but . . . you're coming to the opening night of the musical on the tenth, right?"

"What?" Alice said. "Of course I am. I wouldn't dream of missing it."

"Okay," Cassidy said. "Phew. You've been so busy lately, I wasn't sure you'd make it. You know how to buy tickets, right?" Cassidy prattled on, excitedly telling Alice when the box office would be open for her to buy a ticket and when best to arrive in order to get a good seat and where specifically in the theater to sit. Alice tuned out, because somehow that date sounded familiar, but she wasn't sure exactly why.

Before she could get her thoughts together, Cassidy grabbed Alice by the shoulders. "I don't think I could go out onstage Friday night if I didn't know you were there. I kind of have a big part for someone who just tried out for the first time, and if I do well, who knows, maybe I'll get the lead next time! So I'm excited, but nervous! I'm glad you'll be there rooting for me."

She squeezed Alice's arm and, with a smile, sauntered off to the bathroom to brush her teeth.

Friday night. Alice took her time rinsing off her plate, depositing it in the dishwasher.

Friday night. Alice wiped the crumbs off the marble countertop and dropped them into the sink.

Friday night. Alice switched off the lights underneath the kitchen cabinets.

What was it, exactly, about the night of Friday, November tenth, that was sticking in Alice's mind?

OMIGOSH. The math meet! Nikki's math meet—which Alice had already promised she'd attend—was the same night as the musical!

"You coming or what, slowpoke?" she heard Cassidy call from her bedroom. "I've got beach-luau theme makeup that's just begging for a face to be put on, but *I'm* already doing bright sunflower, so bring your head in here!"

It's okay, Alice coached (and maybe lied to) herself. *I just have to figure out how to be in two places at the same time!*

"Just have to brush my teeth!" Alice called. She took her time walking to her bathroom, which was done up with black-and-white tiles and black-and-white wallpaper to match. She was going to have to figure out a way to act like she wasn't freaking out about what she'd just realized. Lying wasn't fun. And ironically, while she was doing it to try to save both Nikki's and Cassidy's feelings, she was having less fun with both of them because of it.

But what could she do about it? Tell Cassidy about her friendship with Nikki and possibly stay up all night fighting about it? Or tell Nikki, "I know I promised you I would go to your thing, but I can't after all, and P.S., I can't even let Cassidy see me talking to you in the hall"? No, Alice couldn't do either of those things. All she could do was brush her teeth and hope the minty fresh taste would help brush away her bad feelings.

When she finally got to her bedroom, Cassidy was

primping in the mirror, perfecting her cat's-eye with liquid eyeliner.

"Let's get beautiful. Or, I mean, more beautiful." She grinned at Alice. Alice smiled back, but inside she was thinking, *How in the ever-living heck am I going to pull this off?*

CHAPTER 15

TWO FRIENDS, ONE NIGHT

Homeroom was always abuzz right before the weekend, but the classroom was extrafidgety this Friday. Thanksgiving break wasn't too far off, but more important, both the school musical and the math meet were occurring that night. Most kids in class were involved with or had friends who were a part of one of the events, so students chattered about what time they were going, and what they were wearing, if they'd get dinner ahead of time, and whose parents would drive.

"What's on your mind, Kinney?" Aaron Woolsey asked Alice. She had been sitting with her chin in her hands as she contemplated her fate. After a whole week of thinking about it, she still hadn't figured out how to be in two places at the same time. At least both the math meet and the musical took place *in* Lakeside, but the big auditorium (for the musical) and the small auditorium (for the math meet) were at opposite ends of the school. Surely she was going to get busted by either Nikki or Cassidy for not being there when she had said she would be. She couldn't think of an excuse for just staying home, the way she wanted to. Maybe she could fake her own death, or pretend she'd been kidnapped?

"Oh, nothing," Alice said. "I'm, um, just nervous for the math meet."

"But you're not even on the team!" He laughed. "Even though you'd totally be the star of the team, not that I am trying to pressure you to be on it, even though it would totally be fun, no pressure. Pressure, comma, none."

Alice squinted at him. "No. I am not, nor will I ever be on the team, because I like to keep math in class, where it belongs. But I feel like I *am* on the team, after all the cramming I've been doing with Nikki!" Nikki grinned, but when Aaron turned away to talk to Todd, she lowered her head to whisper to Alice.

"Hey," Nikki said. "You don't have to go tonight. It's okay."

"What?" Alice said. "Of course I'll be there. I promised I would."

"But what about the musical?" Nikki asked.

"The musical?" Alice said.

"Alice," Nikki said, rolling her eyes. "You are so smart that you stink at playing dumb. Everyone has been talking about the musical for weeks. There are posters everywhere. *I* would go to it tonight if I weren't in the math meet. And I know that Cassidy's doing a solo in it. She won't stop talking about it during ballet." She smiled wryly.

Alice smiled, exasperated. She couldn't put anything past Nikki. She was probably the smartest person in the Nerd Herd. She was definitely smarter than Alice, who should have taken the chance to get out of the math meet when Nikki gave it to her. But she just couldn't back out of a promise.

"I told you I'd go," Alice said. "And so I will be there. Especially after all that work we put into it! I can't wait to see you rock it."

"All right, people," Ms. Garrity said in her warning voice, which was usually the first of three times she told the students to quiet down before she got really mad and did something drastic like turn off the lights or clap her hands, which were her two favorite ways of displaying that she was serious.

"Doesn't Cassidy want you at her thing?" Nikki asked, lowering her voice to a whisper.

"She'll have so much family there, she won't notice

if I'm gone," Alice said, which was yet another lie. She had celebrated with Cassidy's family after every big performance she'd been a part of—she was practically *a member* of the family. But, as much as Alice hated lying, it almost seemed worth it, based on the big grin on Nikki's face.

"I'm so glad you'll be there," Nikki admitted. "If I do well, it'll be because of you! And if I do badly, I can cry and use your shoulder as a Kleenex." Alice smiled and almost felt embarrassed. Cassidy knew that Alice would be there because they'd *always* been there for each other. Meanwhile, Nikki just seemed so grateful even for the promise of Alice showing up. Alice couldn't let her down, even if Nikki had given her the chance to skip the meet.

All Nikki had needed was someone to listen to her and get to know her, and she came alive. Ever since she had opened up to Alice that morning in homeroom, she had started to speak up more in class. She joked around and even sat at the Nerd Herd table sometimes, when she wasn't cramming for the math meet. Nikki was a great girl and getting greater the more people had the chance to see it.

If only Cassidy could be one of those people. Alice wanted so badly to be a good friend to both girls—but it was pretty hard, especially since there wouldn't be any good chances for Alice to get the two girls together until after the musical and math meet were over—both required its students to eat lunch and practice at the same time. *Afterwards,* Alice promised herself, *I can finally bring my two good friends together. And it'll be awesome . . . I hope!*

"Great," Nikki said, grinning hugely and putting her arm around Alice's shoulders for a spur-of-the-moment squeeze. "I'll see you tonight! Maybe we can go to Walker Bros. afterwards to celebrate!"

"But you haven't even won yet!" Alice laughed.

"Uh, isn't chocolate chip pancakes victory enough?" said Nikki.

Alice headed to the cafeteria to eat with . . . well, she'd find out. It seemed like all of her friends were either spending lunch break rehearsing for the musical or practicing for the math meet. In the hall, she did get the chance to catch Cass before she rushed out of class to the auditorium for one last dress rehearsal.

"You'll do great tonight!" Alice said, giving Cassidy a hug as well as the notebook. What she had really wanted to write in it was something along the lines of *I'm really stuck in a bind: I know two great girls and I don't want to let either of them down. What advice do you have for your best friend?* But Alice wasn't ready to come clean, so instead she drew a rendition of what she imagined the musical would look like, with Cassidy in the spotlight onstage, lots of tiny backup dancers around her, and a stick-figure Alice in the audience cheering "YAY!" *I can't wait for your big moment!* Alice had written at the bottom.

"I hope so!" Cassidy said, both her eyes and grin wide as she shook some nerves out of her hands. "It's like with ballet. I'm always nervous until we get going."

"And just like ballet, it'll be great," Alice said. "I can't wait to watch you be awesome!"

"Remember where to sit, right?" Cassidy said.

"Row fifteen, seat A for Alice," Alice recited. Cassidy had made sure the box office would save her a special seat.

"That's the one!" Cassidy said. "I'll see you tonight!" She gave Alice one last hug before she skipped off down the hall.

I sure hope I can pull this off, thought Alice.

CHAPTER 16

SHOWTIME

"Whoa there, boss," Alice's dad said that evening, as Alice helped herself to her second huge helping of her mom's baked ziti. "Some of us like pasta too. What are you, carbo loading?"

"Sort of," Alice said, with her mouth full.

"Come again?" he asked. "I thought you were going to some sort of math party."

"Math *meet*," Alice said. "And yes, I am going."

"I thought you were going to Cassidy's musical." Mrs. Kinney frowned as she served herself some salad.

"I'm going to that too," Alice said. "I promised both of them I would be at their things, but they're at the same time."

"So what are you going to do?"

"Um," Alice said. "I figured I'd go to Cassidy's musical for fifteen minutes, then run across the hall to Nikki's, see that, and then go back." The second she said it out loud, she knew it sounded ridiculous.

"Alice," her mom said in her most Mom voice. "That sounds ridiculous."

Alice ran her hand through her hair. "I know," she said. "But it's the only way I can make things work."

"Is it?" Mrs. Kinney said. "Think hard. Is it really?"

"Mom," Alice said. "Nikki and Cassidy still don't get along. I know, I wish they would, and I will eventually let Cassidy know I'm friends with Nikki—"

"Wait, Nikki knows that you're friends with Cassidy, but Cassidy doesn't know you're friends with Nikki still?" her mom asked, her eyes wide.

"No," Alice said.

"That sounds kind of sneaky, kid," Mr. Kinney said.

"And not very nice to Nikki. Or Cassidy, for that matter," said her mom.

"I thought best girlfriends tell each other everything," said Mr. Kinney.

"What do best boyfriends do?" Mrs. Kinney asked her husband.

"Tell each other nothing," he said. "Sit around and, you know, talk sports. Pump iron."

Mrs. Kinney smiled and rolled her eyes. "Just tell Cassidy the truth, Alice," she said. "No more deception."

"But what if I make Cassidy mad and she doesn't

want to be my friend anymore?" Alice asked.

"If Cassidy's your true friend, she'll understand— even if she's mad at first," Alice's mom said. "I think you're scared that she'll be upset to find out you have more than one good friend, but doesn't *she* have friends who are in the musical?" Alice frowned and stabbed her last noodle with a fork. It was true, but that didn't bug Alice. Much.

Whatever happened, Alice didn't want to ruin Nikki's or Cassidy's nights with a truth bomb. She'd finally come clean *after* the weekend, after things had died down.

What on earth did one wear to both a musical *and* a math meet, anyway? Alice debated in front of her closet for more minutes than she should have, just delaying the moment until she had to go down to school and run around like a chicken with her head cut off. She knew things would probably be fine, but still, they'd feel a lot finer if she could just sit in one place for the evening. Finally she opted for a sparkly black turtleneck sweater, a preppy blue plaid skirt, gray tights, and some black patent leather flats, so she could run the halls comfortably.

The ride to school with her dad was silent. He

whistled along to the classic-rock station, but she could sense that he wanted to say something (but maybe he could also sense that she didn't want him to).

"Good luck, double agent," Mr. Kinney said, giving her a kiss. "I hope you have fun, whatever goes down."

"Thanks, Dad," she said, and scooted out of the car. Since he had dropped her off at the south exit, which was closer to the small auditorium, she figured she'd start off at the math meet. Plus, Nikki didn't have to hide backstage before the meet began, unlike Cassidy.

The gym, lined with chairs for spectators, was decently full for a Friday night math meet, but Alice was able to grab a seat on the aisle near the exit for a quick getaway. The math team milled around near the front of the staging area in their black-and-red team T-shirts, and Alice strained her neck to make eye contact with Nikki before they started. Nikki finally looked up and spotted her.

"Good luck!" Alice mouthed, and gave her friend a thumbs-up. Nikki grinned sheepishly, sticking out her tongue as she held her too-large T-shirt out in front of her, as if to say, "I can't believe I have to wear this!" But she looked thrilled to see Alice.

Good, Alice thought, relieved. *She's seen me, and she knows I'm here.* Once the house lights went down to start the competition, she slipped out—checking first with one of the students working the door to make sure she'd be able to get back in.

She dashed down the hall to the auditorium, which was packed with students and parents excited to see the show. Alice was impressed as spotlights swirled across the stage and the band played the show's opening notes. This was sort of a bigger deal than she had expected! No wonder Cassidy had been so excited to be a part of it.

A big group number kicked off the musical, but then when the scene ended, Evie and April entered the stage on either side of Cassidy, who looked amazing in a fun silver-and-black tutu, black leggings, and black crop top. Before Alice could cheer, a few other whoops went out in the audience—once again, Alice had to share her best friend with a lot of people, but that wasn't something new. It was just the size of the crowd that she was getting used to.

Alice instead put her fingers in her mouth and let out a loud *weeah-wee!* whistle. When Alice was little and would play over in Cassidy's backyard, Mr. Kinney would use that whistle to call Alice back home. Over time, he had shown them both how to whistle as loud and as clear as he did. Cassidy smiled from ear to ear at the cheering. The girls recited their few lines before they were joined onstage by the seventh and eighth graders who were the main stars of the show.

Alice felt like it was safe to head back out to the math meet, since she knew that Cassidy's solo wasn't until close to the end of the performance. She ducked out of her seat and crouch-ran up the aisle to the back of the theater to try not to disturb the other people in the audience.

Once outside, Alice walked briskly down to the other end of the hall and nearly bumped—hard—into Cassidy's older brother, David, who was walking out of the boys' room.

"Hey, Dingus!" he said, smiling. "What are you doing out here?"

"Oh, just using the bathroom, same as you!" she said. "Obviously."

"Obviously," he said, smiling. "But isn't the bathroom right there?" He pointed to the girls' room, which was behind Alice.

"Oh, yeah," she said. "You know, I was just all excited from seeing Cassidy onstage."

"I bet you're not as excited about Cassidy being onstage as Cassidy is," he smiled, revealing one single adorable dimple on his cheek. "You're a good friend."

Alice beamed. Cassidy would kill her if she ever said what she really thought about her big brother—which was that he was nice *and* cute.

"Well, see you after the show," David said, and headed back to the auditorium. Alice realized that if he looked back, he'd either see her standing there awkwardly or scooting down to the small auditorium, so she had to follow through with using the girls' room. *Aargh, I'm wasting time!* Alice thought as she ran her hands under the water. Once she was sure David had gone back into the musical, she speed-walked down to the gym.

The second she put her hand on the door handle, though, she heard a burst of applause and cheers. Alice sneaked into her chair just in time to see Nikki walking back to her seat, a small, proud smile on her face. *Ack!* If it hadn't been for David, Alice would have seen Nikki score a point for the team. Alice waved, but she was sure Nikki couldn't see her place there in the seats.

The next two students got up to face each other, and Alice realized it'd be a little while again before Nikki was up, so again she left the room as quietly as she could and ran back to the auditorium. When she reached her seat, she pulled her collar away from her neck to give herself some air. All this running around was making her hot!

After a few minutes, she realized that she was watching a seemingly never-ending dance number that Cassidy was not in (which was good; it involved Hula-Hoops and streamers and looked cheesier than anything Cassidy would have ever wanted to be involved with). Alice bounced her knee impatiently.

One scene, two scenes, three scenes. Alice waited and waited for Cassidy to appear onstage for her solo but was only rewarded with some more songs and awkward dialogue and the feeling that she was probably missing another one of Nikki's big moments. She finally ran back to the gym, only to hear the applause again, this time before she even reached the door. She rushed through the door to see Nikki sitting down again. "GO, NIKKI!" she yelled, just to be safe.

To Alice's horror, a few stern faces (including Nikki's parents, eek!) turned around to glare at her. Maybe yelling wasn't encouraged at the math meet until the end? Or maybe Nikki hadn't gotten the problem right? Alice was getting too flustered to even care. She'd worry about it later.

She dashed back to the auditorium, determined

not to miss another moment. Unfortunately for Alice, apparently the janitors had decided to wax the school's pistachio-green floors earlier in the evening, and she found herself sliding on her otherwise cute-and-comfortable flats at the halfway point. In a weird way, for a few seconds, it was almost fun, like she was scooting around on the Turners' hardwood floors in her socks. Until. . . . her ankle twisted out from under her painfully, and she crashed to the floor.

"Point: Nikki Wilcox. Team Lakeside wins!" Alice heard from the south side of the school, just as she heard Cassidy's voice singing out pure and clean—her solo. Applause burst out in stereo from both ends of the hall, echoing down to Alice, making her feel like everyone in the school was sarcastically clapping for her fall and the fact that she had ended up missing both of her friends' big moments. Ouch.

CHAPTER 17

MOMENT OF TRUTH

Was it possible to actually die of embarrassment? Because Alice not only felt like she might, she *hoped* she might. Being dead might actually be better than this. She tried to get up and go . . . somewhere—either auditorium, or preferably home under the covers, or maybe just a cave somewhere on the other side of the world where nobody could find her, but she couldn't get up.

After a few minutes, when both the musical and the math meet had let out, happy families and friends streamed out of both ends of the hall just in time to see Alice sprawled on the floor, holding her sore ankle.

"Are you okay?" asked at least three moms, crouching down in concern before she even had a moment to try to stand up. She felt hot and embarrassed and just wanted to be alone.

"Hey," said a voice close to her, and Alice turned

to see Nikki kneeling next to her. "You sure do like to cause a scene wherever you go, huh?" she asked. "First Walker Bros., now this."

"You know me." Alice laughed.

Nikki's parents walked up. "Alice! Is everything all right?" asked Nikki's mom.

Alice waved weakly. "I'm fine. Just clumsy and embarrassed. I just need a second to find my pride down here somewhere."

"All right, if you say so. Nikki, are you coming with us?"

"I was thinking I'd go out with everyone for ice cream," Nikki said. "To celebrate."

"Are you sure?" said her mom. "We can just get ice cream on the way home."

"I'll be fine, Mom," Nikki said firmly. "I'll be home by eight-thirty. I can get a ride." Dr. and Dr. Wilcox both looked doubtful, but to Alice's surprise, they drifted off towards the doors.

"Seriously, are you okay?" asked Nikki, focusing again on Alice.

"I'm pretty sure I'm fine," Alice said, then noticed the rest of the math team milling around in the hall, high-fiving. "But who cares about me? How are *you*?"

"I answered the meet-winning question!" crowed

Nikki. "It was about the volume of a sphere, which I wouldn't have known if it wasn't for our study session at Walker Bros."

"That's awesome!" said Alice.

"Did you see me?" asked Nikki hopefully.

Alice could do a lot of things, but she didn't have it in her to sit on the floor like a fool and lie at the same time. It was time to finally be honest.

"No," Alice said, grateful that finally some of the crowd was dispersing. "I'm really sorry."

"It's okay," Nikki said. "I heard you cheering for me, and it meant a lot that you were just there at all."

"So *that's* where you were," Alice heard another voice from above. Cassidy stood across from Nikki, back in her street clothes, but either her face was flushed with anger or she was still wearing her stage makeup. Either way, her face was red and she looked mad.

"Cass—" Alice said weakly.

"You were too busy with *her* to come to my show?" Cassidy fumed. "You said you'd see my solo. You lied to me!"

"I was there," Alice said in a small voice. "Didn't you hear me whistle?"

"That was in the first act. What did you do, sneak out? If you had been there, you would've seen that they brought the house lights up at the end of the show for the big dance number at the end. I wanted it to be a surprise," Cassidy said, her eyes filling up with tears. "Everyone with a solo got to pull someone out of the audience to dance onstage at the end of the show. That's why I put you in that special seat—so I could find you. I missed half the number because I was down in the seats looking for you, Alice. It was supposed to be the best part of the show—and instead you were with *her*?" she asked, gesturing to Nikki.

Alice felt heartbroken. The whole time she was worrying that Cassidy was forgetting her, becoming closer with the other kids from the musical, she was planning this surprise for her. Alice stood up unsteadily, favoring her uninjured ankle. She'd be able to hop away on it, but she could tell the other leg was going to be sore the next day.

"I can't believe you chose *her* over me," Cassidy said, pointing dramatically at Nikki's face. Nikki stared at Cassidy for a moment. Like that morning in homeroom when she had cried in front of Alice, her face turned red, and she ran off to the group of Nerd Herders and mathletes getting ready for celebratory ice cream. In moments, the halls were empty, and it was just Alice and Cassidy.

"That was mean of you, Cassidy," Alice said in a low voice. It was time to be real. "I was definitely a jerk, but Nikki didn't do anything to you."

"Hello, do you have amnesia?" said Cassidy. She began ticking off the crimes Nikki had committed against her on her fingers. "She was mean to me in ballet. She's too good to talk to anyone on the bus. She was mean to your boy Aaron. She doesn't want to be a part of your Nerd Herd. She was rude to you, if you don't remember—and now she's stolen my best friend."

"Cass, she's not like that! She's just really shy—you'd know if you'd try to talk to her. Just give her a chance!"

"Why should I give the girl who's stealing my best friend away from me a chance?" Cassidy cried. "Her and your whole Nerd Herd. You think you're better than me since you got into honors classes and I didn't! And hanging out with Nikki just proves it."

And with that, Cassidy ran back to the theater, with Alice in the middle of the hall, by herself, left to figure out which entrance to limp to in order to get a ride home.

CHAPTER 18

AFTER-MATH

It was warm for a November night, and humid. A fine mist created a halo around the school's floodlights as Alice sat on the cement steps, waiting for her dad to come and pick her up. She breathed in the damp air and thought about what had happened.

She would never have figured that popular, outgoing Cassidy would ever feel threatened by anyone as silly and dorky as the Nerd Herd. She also didn't expect to see Nikki stand up to her parents like that either.

"How did everything go?" Alice's dad asked when he came to get her. "Did you manage to be everything to everybody?"

"Uh, not exactly," Alice said, and confessed everything to her dad, who, thank goodness, managed not to say "I told you so" a single time.

"I bet you want to go home and recover from all that drama," her dad said.

"Yeah," Alice said, but then she got an idea. Suddenly, she felt a whole lot better. "Can we actually stop at the Jewel first?"

"Anything for my favorite client," said her dad, touching an imaginary limo driver's cap. Alice smiled in the dark.

"I'll just be a sec," she said, and ducked into the brightly lit but mostly empty grocery store once they pulled up. She grabbed a small but colorful bouquet of flowers and, for her dad, since he was a good sport, a pint of dulce de leche ice cream.

"You didn't have to get me flowers!" said her dad when she got back in the car.

"These aren't for you, silly," she said. "This is for you!" She held up the ice cream.

"I take back everything I ever said about you, Alice," he said. "You're not so bad after all."

"Thanks," she said. "I have one more favor to ask, though," Alice said, as they pulled up to their street. "Can I stop over at Cassidy's place? I know it's late, but I won't be gone long."

"Sure thing," her dad said, turning off the ignition. "Be home in an hour. I'll let your mom know."

Alice took the flowers and walked across the street. The lights were still on in the Turners' kitchen, which meant the family was still up celebrating Cassidy's musical, like they did with her ballet recitals. Alice just hoped that this time she wouldn't be turned away.

"Hi, honey!" Mrs. Turner said after Alice knocked on the door. *Good,* Alice thought. *At least Cassidy hasn't told them all that I'm the worst and turned them all against me.* "Come on in! We're just toasting Cassidy's show with some cupcakes and sparkling cider."

"Sure," said Alice, although she wasn't totally convinced Cassidy wouldn't smash a cupcake into her hair and throw the cider in her face.

"Hi," Alice said to Cassidy, who was sitting primly on one of the high chairs at the kitchen bar.

"Hi," Cassidy said warily to Alice. "What do you have there behind your back?"

Alice presented the flowers. "These are for you. To say congratulations. And I'm sorry."

Cassidy smiled and breathed in the pink daisies' scent. "They're beautiful," she said. She put a cupcake on a plate and extended it to Alice as another peace offering. "This is for you. To say I'm sorry too."

Alice pretended to wrinkle her nose. "Just vanilla? No Funfetti?" She took a bite while she and Cassidy smiled at each other awkwardly and ate their cupcakes in silence. Alice wasn't sure where things would go from here, but it was a start. A delicious start.

"Girls, make sure you get a look at the moon before you say good night," said Mrs. Turner, lingering at the top of the stairs before heading to the rec room to watch TV with Mr. Turner. "It's huge and orange and amazing."

"Want to go check it out?" asked Cassidy.

"Sure," said Alice. She pulled on her green parka, and Cassidy grabbed her red-and-black jacket. She slid open the heavy glass patio door, and the two headed for the swinging seat that they always chose when they sat outside in Cassidy's yard together. Alice couldn't even remember the last time they'd sat out back.

"Oh, wow," whispered Cassidy, and Alice gasped. The moon, which usually looked tiny and faraway, hung huge and low and close over the lake, casting an orange light that reflected on the still water. Some stray wispy clouds lingered in the sky, drawing spooky lines like cobwebs across the huge moon's face. The girls sat in silence for a few minutes, and Alice was grateful that she had something so much bigger than a school musical or honors classes to look at and think about.

"I was really out of line," Cassidy finally said. "Over

at the school. I'm sorry. Are you okay, by the way? I never even asked."

"I'm fine," Alice said. "Mostly just embarrassed. Both because I fell down, and because of my harebrained scheme. I don't know what I was thinking."

"Yeah, what *were* you thinking?" Cassidy said with a laugh.

"So here's the deal," Alice said. She drew a deep breath and finally told Cassidy about the day that Nikki had cried in front of her, going to her house, eating at Walker Bros. with her, everything.

"But I was scared to tell you," Alice said. "Because you *so* didn't like her. And also . . . I didn't say anything at the time, but it felt kind of weird knowing that you were going to the mall, and to get ice cream, and all that other stuff, with the kids from the musical. Without me."

"That's kinda how I felt when I came over and you had the Nerd Herders over," Cassidy admitted.

"Yeah," Alice said. "And since things were already weird, I couldn't find a way or time to say, 'Hey, I know we're not spending much time together, but do you know who I *do* hang out with now is Negative Nikki Wilcox!" Alice took another breath while Cassidy nodded at her to go on.

"Things felt different after I got into honors classes. You have to believe me, I didn't *want* to be separate from you. But I didn't have a choice. And I felt, deep down, like you thought I was choosing *not* to be with you." Alice finally exhaled.

"Okay," Cassidy said. "Truth time?"

"Truth time," said Alice.

"When you got into honors classes, I felt, well, kind of dumb in comparison. And it's taken me awhile to get over that. I didn't think I cared about being asked to join honors until you got asked and I didn't," she said, holding up a hand to Alice, who was about to protest. "I know, I'm not dumb. But still, we grew up doing *everything together*, and when you got moved to a separate class for separate smarties, I felt sad about it. And yeah, I guess a little bit angry. And I took it out on you and Nikki too."

"So you felt kind of how I did when you did the school musical and didn't even ask me," Alice said. "I guess I was worried that you didn't think you needed me anymore, with all your other friends from the musical and in your classes."

"See," Cassidy said, "in a weird way that makes me feel better—that it's weird for you too when I do something separate."

"I guess . . . ," Alice said, toying with one of the wooden toggles on her coat. "Isn't it kind of a good thing, that we can still be best friends and do different things and have separate relationships too?"

Cassidy nodded. "It'll give us more things to talk about. Even if we don't see each other quite as much, we'll still find a way to catch up. And also, Alice? I need to tell you this more, but I'm *proud* of you for being in honors classes. I love that my best friend is so nice and pretty but also so *smart*."

Alice felt warm all over. "I feel like we needed to have this talk way earlier."

"True," said Cassidy. "Let's just be honest with each other from now on."

"I'll try," said Alice.

"And I promise not to just assume that you may or may not want to do something I'm doing," said Cassidy. "No joke, you would have had fun doing stagecraft for the musical. Everybody was messing around and having fun while they were building sets. It was awesome!"

"I could have done that," mused Alice. "As long as it didn't actually mean going onstage." After a moment, she asked Cassidy, "What's it like being onstage, in the spotlight?"

"It's terrifying," admitted Cassidy. "But I love it. It

feels like jumping off the high dive. Once I've done it, I feel so proud of myself." Alice thought to herself about the one time she had climbed up the high dive at the community pool, only, in shame, to walk backwards back down the ladder, too chicken to take the plunge. It was amazing that Cassidy could be so brave about some things but still be insecure about others.

"Can you promise me one more thing?" asked Alice.

"What's that?"

"Will you try to just meet Nikki?" Alice asked. "You don't have to be good friends with her, but just give her a chance."

"Yes. This is the new and improved Cassidy," Cass said, pointing to herself. "I would like to hang out with the new and improved Alice."

"She's getting there," Alice said. She leaned her head on Cassidy's shoulder, and they looked at the moon again, which now was rising higher into the sky, getting smaller and lighter.

Back at Alice's house, her mom just "happened" to be getting a mug of hot chocolate when Alice got home. Alice pretended her mom wasn't just waiting up for her.

"Oh, hi," her mom said. With her makeup still on from the workday, but in her white pajamas and blue terrycloth robe, her mom looked like a model from one of the catalogs Alice and Cass pored through. "Your dad filled me in on everything. Are you okay?"

"Yeah," said Alice, getting one of the painted blue ceramic mugs from the cabinet for herself. "Finally. Thank goodness." Alice tore open an envelope of chocolate powder, and her mom poured her some hot water. Alice blew impatiently on the liquid. The worst thing about hot chocolate was that you couldn't just drink it right away.

"You were right," Alice admitted while waiting for her hot chocolate to cool. "I should have just been honest with Cassidy from the get-go."

"Don't beat yourself up," said her mom. "I understand what it's like to be afraid to hurt someone's feelings."

"You do?" Alice asked.

"Sure," her mom said, and smiled. "Why do you think moms know best? It's from experience!" While Alice finally drank her hot chocolate, her mom told her a few stories about fights with friends when she was younger. Alice was amazed. It sounded like friendships really didn't change that much over the years.

After brushing her teeth and washing her face and putting on her pajamas, Alice was exhausted, but she wanted to do one last thing before falling into her fluffy white comforter.

She booted up her computer. Just as she had hoped, she saw that Nikki was online.

AISFORALICE: Hi.

NKWLCX: Hey.

AISFORALICE: So . . .

AISFORALICE: I already said it, I know, but I'm really sorry I missed your big win tonight.

NKWLCX: And I already said it's fine!

AISFORALICE: No, it's not. I told you I would be there and I wasn't. I was trying to be in two places at once.

NKWLCX: Well . . .

NKWLCX: Thanks for saying that.

AISFORALICE: And also . . .

NKWLCX: ?

AISFORALICE: I know Cassidy feels bad about blowing up at you the way she did.

NKWLCX: Oh.

NKWLCX: It's fine. Whatever.

NKWLCX: . . . I know she's not my biggest fan.

AISFORALICE: Hey, I wouldn't tell you that Cassidy felt bad if she didn't feel bad. I would like you two to try to be friends.

NKWLCX: Do you think it's possible?

AISFORALICE: I think it's definitely possible. Cassidy is going to try.

NKWLCX: Cool.

NKWLCX: Then I will too. ☺

Alice finally crawled into bed. She spent a few minutes awake trying to figure out what the best way to get Nikki and Cassidy to bond would be. Maybe a walk along the lake? But it was getting cold. Lunch at Walker Bros.? It was kind of noisy there. Maybe a movie? But you can never really talk at a movie. Despite her buzzing mind, Alice fell asleep and, for what seemed like the first time in weeks, slept soundly.

COME TOGETHER

A week later, Alice still hadn't figured out the perfect way for Cassidy and Nikki to discover their common ground, but at least she didn't feel like she was living a double life anymore. Cassidy said, "Hi, Nerd Herd!" to the entire honors group (including Nikki) when the classes switched rooms between periods, and in the notebook, she told Alice that Nikki had started spending a bit more time after ballet.

She's not saying a lot, but I think she's just warming up to us. It's nice that she's part of the group, Cassidy wrote. With the musical over, they now had more time to write and to fill up the last few pages of the notebook.

But how could Alice get Cassidy and Nikki to get to know each other the way she knew them?

"All right, guys, this is a tough one," Mr. Nichols announced in English. "If you *don't* cry, I'm probably going to mark you down a grade." He passed out the latest book they were to study: *Old Yeller*.

"Oh jeez," said Aaron Woolsey, looking at the cover, which featured a very sad-looking yellow Labrador. "I'm worried I'm going to cry right now."

"Crying gets you extra credit," said Mr. Nichols, and soon the room was filled with the exaggerated boo hoos of everyone pretending to cry.

Alice grinned. No matter how sad the book was, she had a feeling that her dog allergy would probably make it easier for her to read than everyone else.

Suddenly, inspiration struck. Why hadn't she thought of this before? It was so obvious!

"Hey," she said, tapping Nikki on the shoulder. She was joking around with Todd Tian as they stood up to head to the next class. "Heads up. We're heading to Cassidy's house after school today."

"Oh, we are, are we?" asked Nikki, raising one eyebrow.

"Yes," said Alice.

"Are you *sure*?" Nikki asked again.

"Trust me," Alice said, flashing a grin. She was super excited and quickly scribbled a note to Cassidy in the notebook.

It's a Nerd Herd invasion at your house after school today, and I want to invite a very special, slobbery guest. P.S. I hope that's okay. P.P.S. Hi!

"What's the word, Herd?" Cassidy called out as her class and honors classes switched rooms for the period.

"Here," said Alice, handing her the notebook, which was almost full by now. "Make sure you read it before the end of the day. Promise?"

"Sure," said Cassidy. "Is everything okay?"

"It's going to be!" said Alice, smiling mysteriously, before heading into biology.

Nikki and Alice had agreed earlier in the month to volunteer to wash out the lab equipment after school, so they took the late bus home. There was only a half sun left over the horizon by the time they reached Alice's street and started walking to Cassidy's house.

"Wait, you live *right across the street* from Cassidy?" asked Nikki.

"Yep," Alice answered. "It's pretty awesome."

"No wonder you two are so tight," said Nikki. "Okay, so just one more time . . . are you sure it's all right that I'm coming over?"

"Why won't you trust me?" Alice asked. "I don't say things I don't mean. Anymore." With a smile she rang the doorbell. Immediately Alice heard Bagel yipping and scrabbling about on the foyer's wooden floor.

Nikki turned to Alice, her face alight. "Cassidy has a dog?" she exclaimed. "Oh my gosh, I love dogs."

"I know," said Alice. "Friends tend to remember these types of things."

Nikki stared down at her booted feet bashfully but then looked up when she heard the key turning in the lock. There stood Cassidy, smiling and wearing an oversize moss-green sweater over pale pink jeans, and holding Bagel, who was wiggling around like he wanted to take flight.

"Come in!" she said. "Here, take this," she told Nikki, once they were in from the cold. Cassidy dumped Bagel into her arms like she'd done it a thousand times before. "I hear you like dogs," she said. "That's good, because Bagel likes people who like dogs. You're not *allergic*, are you?" she said, casting a sly look at Alice, who stuck out her tongue.

"I don't think so," Nikki said, crouching down on the Oriental rug so she could give Bagel belly rubs. "And even if I was, I wouldn't care. Oh, I love him!"

"If you keep giving him attention, he'll love you right back," Cassidy said.

"I can't stop petting him. He's so soft!" said Nikki. She petted Bagel so much that a tuft of his hair wafted up in the air, which made Alice sneeze. Nikki and Cassidy laughed. Alice grinned, even though she really wanted a Kleenex. Maybe this would go okay after all.

The girls spent the last hour or so of daylight in Cassidy's big backyard while she and Nikki threw toys for Bagel to fetch. Alice marveled at how energetic he was: he ran after tennis balls, rings, even a plastic bagel. Each time he ran back to Nikki or Cassidy, they had to jump out of his way so he didn't get muddy paw prints on their legs. Alice, of course, had to sit a little ways away from the two of them, because the telltale itching on the underside of her forearms meant that she wasn't that far away from a full-blown allergy attack. She didn't mind, though. She liked listening to Nikki and Cassidy talk about dogs and ballet.

"When's the next musical?" Nikki asked.

"Next semester," answered Cassidy. "I think they're doing *Grease*."

"I love *Grease*!" said Nikki, hurling the ball to the

opposite end of the yard. "Although to be honest, I always secretly wanted to be a T-Bird more than a Pink Lady. Is that weird?"

"I feel exactly the same way!" said Cassidy. "They had better songs and also, I look much better in black than pink."

"I didn't know you sang, Nikki," Alice called out.

"Well, a little," said Nikki. "In choir at church."

"But if you do *Grease*, what about the math team?" Alice asked.

"I'm not sure yet!" Nikki said. "I kind of told my parents I'm thinking about quitting the team and trying something else." She shrugged. "And believe it or not, they actually didn't keel over."

Alice was filled with pride for her new friend, who seemed to be getting better every day at coming out of her shell and reassuring her parents that she would be okay if she did her own thing.

"What if we started a writing group?" Alice pondered aloud. "We could ask Mr. Nichols to help us start it. And it doesn't have to be just people from the Nerd Herd." She was surprised when this idea fell out of her mouth— she had never actually thought of that idea before—but it could be fun. She had enjoyed Mr. Nichols's class and writing to Cassidy in the notebook so much. Maybe she could take it further. Alice felt like it was maybe time for her to try something new again.

"I think that's a great idea," said Nikki.

Alice heard a shriek and looked over to see Cassidy gasping. Bagel had finally gotten the best of her and put his black paw prints all over her light-colored jeans.

"Oh gosh!" Alice said, standing up, ready to help Cassidy into the house and throw her jeans in the washing machine as fast as possible.

"You know what?" said Cassidy, looking down and laughing. "It doesn't matter." She jumped around and held Bagel's front legs as if they were dancing.

Alice felt like she didn't have to *worry* anymore—about honors, about Cass, or Nikki. They could all just *be* together. What mattered was that they were friends.

CHAPTER 20

A NEW CREW

A sky-blue notebook to signify a brand-new day.
Okay, just kidding, it was the first one I saw. Nikki,
welcome to the notebook.
Pop quiz time!
What is the most delicious fruit?
What's the last thing you watched on TV?
Where was the last scar you got? How did you get
it?
What's your favorite song from <u>Grease</u>?
Fill it out and pass it on to Cassidy!

"Hey, bookworm, aren't you going to go outside?"
Alice, sitting on the cushioned window seat in the
kitchen, looked up from her reading. Her dad had just
come in from a jog, his gray T-shirt dark with sweat,
his hair sticking up above the silly white sweatband he
wore on his forehead. "It's freakishly nice out. In the

sixties at least." He helped himself to a glass of water from the sink and then lay down on the kitchen floor to stretch, taking up nearly the entire room. Alice's mom came in from hanging the winter-themed wreath on the front door.

"I hear it's supposed to be in the thirties tomorrow," she said. "Honey, I hate to say it, but the weather might not be nice again until May."

"Try June," said Mr. Kinney.

"Why do we live here again?" asked Mrs. Kinney. Mr. Kinney pointed to the backyard, where the lawn was a bright green-and-gold carpet thanks to the tiny leaves that had finally finished falling off the trees.

"Oh yeah," said Mrs. Kinney. "That helps."

Alice put her book down next to her and stretched her legs. "I know, I know," she said. "I need to go out before it gets dark."

"Which isn't in that long, by the way," said Mr. Kinney. "Daylight savings and all."

"It's just that I'm really into this book," she said, casting her eyes back down to the cover of her book, which featured a boy, not much older than her, from the chin down, wearing a white T-shirt and a black leather jacket. She was totally engrossed by *The Outsiders* and been trying hard not to develop little crushes on the tough but sensitive Greaser boys. And she wasn't the only one.

When Cassidy spotted Nikki's copy on the lunch table at the cafeteria, she was instantly intrigued—the guys in the book did resemble the T-Birds from *Grease*, after all. So Cassidy decided to read the book too, and was totally engrossed. During the past week, the girls had discussed what they read. When Xia, Evie, and April saw that Nikki, Cassidy, and Alice were all reading the same book, they wanted in on the action too.

Once they were all finished, Nikki had promised to host an epic sleepover so they could all watch the movie version of the book. Xia's copy featured the poster on the cover, and the girls could not get over what young Tom Cruise used to look like. In the meantime, Alice couldn't wrap her head around the fact that the book's author had been only eighteen years old when the book was published. It made her think about trying to start writing her own novel over winter break. So, yeah, she was into *The Outsiders*. But maybe she should go outside while she had her chance.

Ding-dong! As if by magic, the doorbell rang to distract her from her conundrum. Mr. Kinney had started doing walking lunges from the kitchen to the front hall and opened the front door.

"Alice, it's for you!"

When she got to the front door, she saw that it was Cassidy and Nikki—Cass in her red-and-black jacket, Nikki carrying her army-green one over her arm as she tried to control Bagel, who was squirming desperately on the other end of the leash she was holding. Apparently he wanted to come inside and shed all over everything the Kinneys owned.

"What are *you* guys up to?" Alice asked.

"We were going to take Bagel to the beach and let him run around because, as you can see, he has way too much energy. Want to come with?"

"Cassidy invited me over," Nikki said almost apologetically. "I hope it's okay."

"Of course it's okay!" Alice said.

"Oh, um, I meant about your allergies," said Nikki. "I hope it's okay for *you* to hang out."

Alice laughed. She realized she didn't have to worry so much about Nikki—or herself. "Yes, it'll be fine," she said. "Nikki, you just pet Bagel for me."

"Done and done!" Nikki said, squatting down to give Bagel some love.

"Well, hi, Nikki; hi, Cassidy," said Alice's mom.

"Mom, Nikki and Cassidy were taking Bagel for a walk. Can I go with?"

"Of course, get outside while the getting's good," she said. "Just stop letting the leaves get inside the house. I don't feel like vacuuming again."

"Okay, good point," Alice said. "I need to get my jacket. Meet you guys in the back?" She shut the door so Nikki and Cassidy could take Bagel round to the backyard.

"I'm proud of you, honey," Mrs. Kinney said, putting her arm around Alice's shoulders as they walked back to the kitchen.

"Why?" asked Alice, pulling on her light denim jacket for probably the last time until spring next year.

"Because I know it's been a struggle for you to figure out how to balance your school responsibilities and be a good friend, and it seems like you have," she said. "I'm more proud of you for finding a balance than if you had a million friends or got a million straight A's."

"Well, good, because I don't know if it's possible for me to get a million straight A's," said Alice.

"You're a good kid, even if you are a sass mouth," her mom said. "Have fun on the walk."

Alice had skipped down the back steps to join her friends when she heard her mom call to her one more time.

"Girls, wait!" she said. They turned around, and Mrs. Kinney stood with her digital camera in her hand. "You all look so happy and it's such a nice day—let me take a picture."

"Will you send me a copy, Mrs. Kinney?" said Cassidy. "My mom will want to see this."

"Me too!" said Nikki.

"Sure!" said Mrs. Kinney. "Now get together."

Alice felt Cassidy's and Nikki's arms around her waist, and she thought of the first day of school, feeling grateful that she wasn't as nervous anymore, either about classes or her friendship with Cassidy.

"Ready?" said Mrs. Kinney. "One, two—"

"Wait!" said Nikki. "Bagel has to be in the picture too!" Before Alice could suggest an appropriate pose that would incorporate the four of them, Nikki yelled "Here!" and thrust Bagel into her arms. Bagel, thrilled that for once Alice was giving him some attention, nuzzled her neck and licked her face. Alice laughed, even though it was kind of gross.

"Are you *sure* you're allergic?" Cassidy asked for the millionth time. As if on cue, Alice felt a giant sneeze welling up inside her sinuses. She tried to say, "Mom, wait!" before the camera went off, but before she could,

Nikki tickled her in the ribs, so she knew a big messy laugh-sneeze was coming any second and there was nothing she could do about it. Oh, great.

Aah—aah—choo!

SNAP!

READ ON FOR A SNEAK PEEK
OF PICTURE PERFECT #4: BETWEEN US!

CHAPTER 1

HOW TO HAVE AN EPIC FIRST WEEK OF MIDDLE SCHOOL

Prep
1. *Go to mall with Olivia and check out what seventh and eighth graders are wearing. Then shop!*
2. *Start getting up at time you need to get up for school. No oversleeping. (Walking in late—yikes.)*
3. *Practice on combination lock.*
4. *Study map of school.*
5. *Organize school supplies.*
6. *Buy mints for locker.*

When School Starts
1. *Eat breakfast so stomach won't grumble.*
2. *Meet one person you didn't go to elementary school with.*
3. *Smile at people (but not like an insane clown girl).*
4. *Write down assignments.*

5. Find out about clubs.

6. Remind Oh to use a straw so she won't spill!

7. Relax!!!!!

"I'm not sure you get to check off number seven," Olivia told her best friend.

"Why?" Bailey protested. Her fingers were itching to check off the last item on her Epic First Week list.

"How relaxed can you be if you have to have a list that tells you to be relaxed?" Olivia asked.

"Have you forgotten who you're talking to?" Bailey exclaimed, her voice rising. "Lists make me more relaxed than anything."

Olivia shook her head, setting her dark brown curls bouncing. "I just wanted to see how unrelaxed you'd get if you thought you'd have to leave something unchecked. You should have heard yourself squeak. It was like a mouse on helium."

"You're bad," Bailey told her, trying not to laugh. "A bad, bad friend." Bailey made an extrabig check next to number seven.

"Just trying to help you impulsify a little. You might miss something good if you're always looking at a list," Olivia told her.

Bailey and Olivia were so different. Oh didn't like

to plan. She didn't even like basic rules, such as using words that were actually in the dictionary.

"I can impulsify!" Bailey looked around, trying to think of a way to prove it. "Look! I'm . . . I'm *sing*-ing in pub-*lic*." She warbled the last few words, and didn't care that a couple people turned around and stared at her.

Olivia gave a laugh that turned into a snort. "I can't believe you did that. I was horrifyingly close to spraying blueberry soda out of my nose."

"It would have been your own fault," Bailey teased. She took a sip of her raspberry drink. She and Olivia always went to Emmy's for Italian sodas when they had something to celebrate, and completing their first week of middle school was definitely what Olivia would call whoop-whoop worthy.

As different as they were, the two of them had been friends since the second grade. Somehow Bailey's love of planning and Olivia's willingness to try anything were a perfect combination. No matter how much time they spent together, they always wanted to be together more.

Bailey could probably fill a whole notebook with all the ways Olivia was an awesome friend. Her birthday was coming up in about a month. Maybe Bailey would make that list as part of her present. Olivia couldn't have a problem with a list like that!

"So next week at school, we should—" Bailey was interrupted by her cell clucking. She'd let Olivia set the ringtones. She checked it.

need you home. big news!

Bailey showed the text to Olivia. "I wonder what's up," Olivia said.

"Could be anything," Bailey answered. "Remember that text that said I had to get home ASAP, and it was because the first rosebud of the year was opening on one of her bushes?"

"That was cool. I love your mom," Olivia told her.

"Do you want to come with me?" Bailey asked. "Oh, wait. You can't. You've got karate." Olivia kept trying new sports to see if there was one where her klutziness wasn't a problem. Last year she'd taken dance. Kind of a disaster.

Olivia jumped up so fast she almost tipped over her chair. "I've got karate! I forgot!"

Bailey checked the time on her phone. "You're good. You have twenty-four minutes."

"Text me and tell me what the big news is," Olivia said as Bailey slid her notebook into her backpack.

"I will," Bailey promised.